Sweetest Gift

STEPHANIE PERRY MOORE

The Negro National Anthem

Lift every voice and sing
Till earth and heaven ring,
Ring with the harmonies of Liberty;
Let our rejoicing rise
High as the listening skies,
Let it resound loud as the rolling sea.
Sing a song, full of the faith that the dark past has taught us,
Sing a song, full of the hope that the present has brought us,
Facing the rising sun, of our new day begun
Let us march on till victory is won.

So begins the Black National Anthem, by James Weldon Johnson in 1900. Lift Every Voice is the name of the joint imprint of The Institute for Black Family Development and Moody Publishers, a division of the Moody Bible Institute.

Our vision is to advance the cause of Christ through publishing African-American Christians who educate, edify, and disciple Christians in the church community through quality books written for African-Americans.

The Institute for Black Family Development is a national Christian organization. It offers degreed and non-degreed training nationally and internationally to established and emerging leaders from churches and Christian organizations. To learn more about The Institute for Black Family Development, write us at:

The Institute for Black Family Development
15151 Faust
Detroit, MI 48223

Since 1984, Moody Publishers has been dedicated to equip and motivate people to advance the cause of Christ by publishing evangelical Christian literature and other media for all ages, around the world. Because we are a ministry of the Moody Bible Institute of Chicago, a portion of the proceeds from the sale of this book go to train the next generation of Christian leaders.

Moody Publishers
c/o Moody Publishers Ministries
820 N. LaSalle Blvd.
Chicago, IL 60610

Sweetest Gift

STEPHANIE PERRY MOORE

Library of Congress Cataloging-in-Publication Data is
available.

3 5 7 9 10 8 6 4
Printed in the United States of America

To my handsome godsons

Danton Lynn,
Dakari Jones,
and
Dorian Lee

Every Christmas,
I want to play Santa
and buy you
whatever your hearts desire,
but then I realized that telling
you guys about Jesus Christ
is the sweetest gift I could give you!

May you all grow to be godly men
that love the Lord with all your hearts!

Contents

Acknowledgments

As I sit and wrap gifts this Christmas, I received a special gift in the mail. It was a preview copy of Book 3, Saved Race, in the Payton Skky series. I held it tightly, hugged it, and prayed over it. After all, this was my baby being born. God had used me to do it again. I was humbled. Then I realized I had a deadline for Book 4 that was steadily approaching. Thanks to the support of several people, I made my deadline. This is a small thank you to those who made this work possible.

To my parents, Franklin and Shirley Perry: Teaching me how to have **SELF-ESTEEM** is the sweetest gift you've given me. With it, I believe I can achieve God's plan for my life. How awesome to be born yours!

To my publishing company, Moody Press, particularly Greg Thornton: Your sweet gift is giving me **SELF-ASSURANCE**. By publishing my work, I now know that I know, that I know . . . writing is a part of God's plan for my life. What a blessing to be a part of the Moody team!

To my reading pool, Laurel Basso, Sarah Hunter, Andrea Johnson, Kim Johnson, Tracy Williams, and my assistant, Nakia Austin: You all give me the sweet gift of **SELF-DISCIPLINE**. Being accountable to you by keeping my word and sending five chapters at a time has made me step it up a notch. So fortunate to have good friends like you!

To my author mentors, Marjorie Kimbrough, Robin Jones Gunn, and Victoria Christopher Murray: The sweetest gift you place into my life is giving me your encouragement that helps me become a **SELF-STARTER**. Staying committed to writing every day is now accomplished in my life because of your prayers and influence. Knowing you personally brings me joy!

To my singing group, Joybells, Gloria Clark, Sheldyn Moore, Sydni Moore, and Tyra Whitehead: **SELF-DETERMINATION** is the sweet gift I receive from you every time we practice and record. Your innocence and enthusiasm has allowed me to stay pure in heart and to believe God for miracles. I'm proud of your work on the Camel Praise album!

To my husband, Derrick Moore: **SELF-SATISFACTION** is the sweetest gift you've given me. I feel complete because we are one. How special I feel being yours!

To the reader, wherever you are: You give me **SELF-FULFILLMENT**. Every letter, e-mail, or kind word about my writing life, touches my soul. My living is not in vain because I live my life to help others.

And to my Lord, Jesus Christ: Your sweet gift is that of **SELF-LOVE**. Because the Holy Spirit dwells within me, I adore who I am. I pray every young person learns to feel good about who they are or were created to be.

1

Reliving the Past

ell, Lord," I prayed on my knees in my new dorm room, "this is a little different. Not my cozy room at home. I'm a big girl now. And not that You don't know, but I am very, very nervous. A freshman in college, and although school doesn't start for another week, I don't know if I'll be ready. I am truly nervous. Will I make friends? Maybe all this is stupid. I've been waiting to graduate forever, and I've been waiting to move out and be on my own even longer. Now I've gotten the opportunity, and I don't know if I even want it. Help me. Give me strength. Help me find out who I am so that I can make it on my own."

I had a lot to say to my Father above. I hated being timid, but I was. He could help me, so I prayed on: "No more parents to lean on; it's just me and You. Thanks again for my new roommate, Laurel. Yeah, she's white, but she doesn't seem ditsy; she's cool. Though she seems cool now, living with her might be different . . . just help us. Help me to make You proud in all I do. My ex-boyfriends Dakari and

Tad will be at Georgia, too. Lord, please run interference. Oh, and I pray for my girlfriends, Lynzi, Dymond, and Rain, that wherever they are, Lord, You'll be with them. And for my mom—I know it is hard for her not having me at home. Well, I'm gonna try to sleep for the first time in this bed. Bless Daddy too. Amen."

As I lay back on the bed, I looked over at Laurel. She was knocked out. Such peace seemed to overcome her. However, I couldn't sleep. The last year of my life had been full of so much drama. So I kind of reflected and thought about what had brought me from that point to this one.

It seemed like the craziness started just last August when my boyfriend of three years, Dakari, wanted us to go to his brother's football game. Which is so weird because at the time Dakari and I were driving from Augusta to where we are now, Athens. We went to see his brother, Drake, a senior, play football for Georgia.

Being in my jeep that day, I never would have thought a year would pass, and I would be a freshman at Georgia. I never really gave much thought to where I wanted to go to college, but I knew the University of Georgia was not high on my list. I wanted to go to an HBC, a historically black college. I have two girlfriends that took that route: Dymond, who's at Howard, and Rain, who's at Spelman. I thought I would be at a school like that, not at UGA. But, anyway, Dakari and I were driving, and we pulled off the road at a rest stop. It was kind of isolated, and nobody was there, and one thing led to another, and, boy, were we feeling each other.

It was hot and passionate. Dakari is a real cute brotha and all, but something inside of me said, *No, this is not what I want.* So I pushed him off me and ended the craziness.

I remember him yelling, "What! You don't want this?"

It wasn't that I didn't want it, because I did. But we said we would wait until marriage, and we were only seniors in high school. Actually, our senior year hadn't even started yet. So why tread into forbidden territory?

Dakari said he was cool with it. Little did I know he really wasn't cool with it at all. He was hot, ticked off at me, and our relationship would never be the same. We went on to that game, faked it, I guess. We met his parents up at the college and pretty much had a great time.

Oh, yeah, that's the day I met Tad Taylor. He was another football player who was being recruited by UGA. When I first saw him, *umm*. I didn't even know at that moment that the fascination I felt for him would last and that he'd one day be mine.

Dakari was jealous when he introduced me to Tad because the charming guy kissed my hand. However, at that point, I wanted Dakari to be jealous. He was mad that we didn't go farther. So, hey, if this Tad guy could ruffle his feathers, I played the role. Not that it was all about games, but we were young, and in one whole year, I had done so much growing up.

Fast-forward three days from that moment: Dakari broke up with me on the first day of school for some new chick, Starr Love. What a name; I still can't believe that name. She looked like a star too. She was gorgeous. She had breathtaking, sunrise skin and ginger brown hair that flowed like a river. Her body was way tighter than mine. For three years, I had been the stuff at my school, and now Starr had come along and not only captivated the school but took my man, too. How humbling!

It was hard to swallow. I was so angry at everybody. Perry, my brother, who is two years younger, tried to fight Dakari because he left me for another. I was definitely mad at Dakari. I remember I tried to give it up to him after I found out he had another girlfriend. But I can say I'm glad he turned me down, because here I am still a virgin. Wow! After all that, God helped me stay pure.

I thought I'd never have another boyfriend. I was humiliated by Starr's presence at my school. But amazingly enough, I became homecoming queen. I remember those days so well. Starr had been nominated. I was ticked off; people didn't even know her! I remember that night as if it were yesterday: Her dad, the judge, escorted her out onto the field; and my dad, the car dealer, escorted me.

She mumbled, "Did you see my boyfriend do well in the first half of the game? Now all he needs is for the homecoming queen to be his girlfriend. Oh, I guess that can't be you.'Cause you are no longer the woman in his life."

Her face was cracked and on the ground when they called my name instead of hers. It was great for about five minutes after I won, but when I saw her dancing with Dakari at the homecoming dance, I realized that she had the bigger prize. I really cared for him. We had been tight.

That's when I felt God had let me down. Or so I thought. I had to search within myself, see what I was all about. Gratefully, I learned it was not about a guy. I couldn't find happiness in Dakari. I needed to find happiness in Christ. I think I learned that when the Lord let me run into Tad the weekend I came back up to UGA to visit.

I tried to play hard to get for a while, but I think it was around Christmas when I found out Tad Taylor was from Aiken, South Carolina, which is twenty-five minutes away from my house. Tad Taylor, that chocolate brotha who was after God's own heart, started telling me how much he admired me. He started dating me the way God wants a guy to date one of His girls. It was like night and day compared to my time with Dakari.

It was always weird to me how one day a guy becomes a husband, and he's supposed to lead, when he never did it in a dating relationship the way God expects. Yet a woman is supposed to follow. I guess that's where the whole equally yoked thing comes in. God says that a Christian should only date or marry a Christian. This is so the couple can share common, deep issues of the heart. Maybe if girls would start expecting more from guys that they go out with, then there wouldn't be so much drama. There surely was drama for Tad and me. Even though Tad was a Christian, when we started dating and connecting on that spiritual level, I was attracted to him physically. I just couldn't get around wanting to give it up, and for the wrong reason or the right reason, I was there. Fortunately, Tad was strong enough for the both of us; and there again, God was looking out for me.

So Tad escorted me to my debutante ball, which was fun. I was one of fifty girls presented to society by the Links Organization, which was a group of strong black women that my mom was a part of. I didn't think I'd have an escort, but Tad hooked me up. He escorted me to the ball, and, boy, did we have a ball. By that time—six months later—Dakari was so fed up with Starr that he wanted me back, and I think I wanted him back, too. Drama, drama, drama.

I went down the hall to get a soda out of the machine. The walls of my new surroundings were eerie. Dorm life, ugh! It was nothing like I thought it would be. It wasn't horrible! There were no roaches or anything, but it just wasn't cozy, like home. I didn't think I was going to like it.

When I bent down to get a Coke, I heard a pleasant voice behind me say, "So you can't sleep either?"

When I turned around, it was a face like mine. A timid, stout, coffee-colored girl that seemed just as scared as I was to be there. Without thinking, I hugged her. She must have thought I was weird. I didn't even know what I was thinking. I was just so happy to see another person like me that I hugged her tight. Surely we weren't gonna be the only blacks at UGA. After all, I knew Tad and Dakari. Seeing another black female in the dorm when all I had seen were white faces that mostly hated seeing me there was great. I knew I wasn't welcome, because I overheard my two suite mates talking about how they wished they didn't have to share a bathroom with a black girl. That's probably what the hug was about. Somewhere deep down inside, I was happy to know that I wasn't alone. The Lord had placed someone at school to whom I could relate. I was overjoyed.

"I'm Payton," I said as I released my grasp.

"Payton, hi. I'm Cammie."

"Kammie with a K, or Cammie with a C?" I questioned, seeing her name in my mind.

"Cammie with a C. C-A-M-M-I-E."

"Where are you from, Cammie?"

"Opelika, Alabama."

"Where?" I asked her, unsure I had heard correctly.

"Opelika. You ever heard of Auburn?"

"Yeah, that's another SEC school."

"Well, Opelika is right beside Auburn."

"So why didn't you go to Auburn?"

"Well, I lived there all my life, and I just wanted to get away. A lot of my friends from high school went to Auburn."

"Really? I can understand wanting to get away. How long have you been here?"

"Today's my first day."

"Yeah, me too," I told her.

"You like it?" she asked.

"I don't think so."

"Why'd you hug me?" she asked candidly.

"Girl, I don't know. I guess I was just happy to see another black face. Sorry if I offended you."

"Oh, no, no. Though Opelika has a lot of whites, I can tell these girls up here aren't used to seeing a lot of blacks."

"Tell me about it."

Since her roommate was asleep and mine was asleep,

too, we went over to the front of the dorm into the commons area and sat down. I started telling her about my crazy past and talked about my prom.

"It was crazy," I said. "I was dating one guy, Tad, and I went to his prom, but he had to go somewhere like a Christian retreat or something and couldn't take me to mine. Girl, I was mad. So, my ex-boyfriend, Dakari, wanted to take me, so I went with him. It was a trip! We were prom king and queen. He kissed me, and I liked it. The thing about it was Tad felt so bad that he came to my prom, in a tux and all, and saw me on stage kissing Dakari."

"Are you serious?" she asked.

"Yes. I'm very serious. Talk about drama my senior year. I kind of liked them both. My feelings swung back and forth between the two."

"So what about your girlfriends?"

"I had good girlfriends in school. I miss them. One of my girlfriends, Lynzi, had a hard year."

"What do you mean?" she asked, intrigued by my story.

"Well, she had a boyfriend, Bam."

"Bam?"

"Yeah, that's his nickname. We've called him that for so long I don't even know what his real name is."

"We've got some folks like that in Opelika."

"Lynzi's parents are divorced, so she had issues anyway. I'm so proud of the fact that I'm a virgin that I could just go and scream it off a rooftop. I'm a virgin! But Lynzi is the opposite. I think she lost her virginity at the age of fourteen when her dad moved out. She had a cheatin' boyfriend named Bam. To make a long story short, she thought she was pregnant."

"No, girl, she thought she was pregnant?"

"Yeah, we kind of had a scare. A rumor got around school, and the only people who knew were Bam and me. When it got out, no one thought that Bam would spread a rumor about himself fathering a baby. So Lynzi got mad at me. My other close girlfriend, Dymond, who likes to know everybody's b'ness, got mad at me because I didn't tell her. I had one girlfriend mad at me because she thought I told, and one mad at me because I didn't tell. That was really the first time we had serious best-friend tension.

"I had another friend, Rain, this tall, beautiful girl, who tried to keep the peace, but it wasn't workin' for a while. When it all came out, Bam was the one who told loud-mouthed Dakari who told some football players, and it went on from there. Lynzi had taken some pregnancy tests, and they came out positive."

"So what happened? Did she have an abortion and nobody knew?"

"No, it wasn't nothin' like that. They weren't even pregnancy kits. They were like ovulation predictors or something." I laughed as I told the story.

Cammie was cool. It was neat. I was scared being there, and God provided someone to let me just unleash and talk about stuff that really meant a lot to me. Bringing back up all that stuff allowed me to know that God was watching out for me in more ways than one and more than I ever knew. 'Cause just like He was there then, He's here now.

"Well, that's good she wasn't pregnant," Cammie cut in and reminded me of my place in the story.

"Yes . . . but she wanted to kill herself some months later."

"Why?"

"I don't know. I guess because Bam broke up with her and because of the situation with her parents. We went through this whole thing with drinking, and she hit a tree."

"Is she OK?"

"Yeah. She walked away from that, too," I said, laughing. "I'm not laughing because I think it's funny. I'm laughing because I can't believe all this stuff happened in one year."

17

"Yeah, a lot of stuff did happen to you," Cammie agreed.

I must have been missing home. I was telling a stranger all of my business. Actually, though, talking through everything was somehow therapeutic. I'm glad I went against my character and bared my soul.

"Then as I bounced back and forth from Tad to Dakari, my cousin Pillar from Denver, who's gonna be a senior this year, came to visit. We never were close. I think Tad and Dakari liked her. Maybe they didn't really like her, but they gave her attention. I wanted them both and didn't want her to have either one. Then I let myself get caught up in the wrong guy because Dakari was the one paying her the most attention. We started getting closer again, and the next thing I knew we were in a hotel room, and he wanted to go farther than I was willing to take it. It was not a good scene."

"Oh, my gosh. Did he force himself on you?"

"Something like that, but luckily he stopped. . ."

"And?" Cammie pressed.

"And I realized that though I still care for him, which is stupid, he isn't the one for me."

I hoped those words I was saying to Cammie were the truth. Because Dakari had a way of batting his eyes and saying the right stuff to make any girl fall for him. I hoped that I could remember the words that I was saying to this stranger. I did not need Dakari; he was not the one for me. Whatever might come up in these next four years with us being together at school, I could not allow myself to be swayed his way.

"On the other hand, Tad was there. He understood, and he was cool about it."

"So are y'all together?"

"I don't know. There has been so much damage. Speaking of damage, my friend Lynzi. . ."

"The one who thought she was pregnant?"

"Yeah, she came across this guy, and he assaulted her, too."

"Oh, boy. She must be a wreck."

"Yep, she joined the army. She was supposed to come here with me, but she said she needed a structured environment. She needed to toughen up. Well, I see you yawnin'," I said to Cammie. "What room are you in?"

"Three-twelve," she said.

"I'm on the first floor. I'm in Room 106. We'll have to hook up. My phone is in, but I can't remember the number, plus it's late. Come down tomorrow."

"Yeah, I'll do that," she said.

Speaking from the heart, I told her, "It was nice to meet you."

"You too."

I saw the sun peering through my window. As I looked at the rays, I remembered the events of my first days in the dorm room, when Dakari came over and tried to tell me he was sorry. Sorry for being forceful with me a month earlier!

We went outside because I knew the conversation might not be too pretty. After all, I was furious with Dakari. I told him no, he kept going. A part of me didn't know if I could forgive him. When he came to my new surroundings and wanted forgiveness, I just lost it. I didn't want him to touch me; I didn't want him to say anything to me. When Tad walked up on the situation, the two of them got into it. They started scuffling; one thing led to another, and my dorm room window got busted. Drama, yet again. I was happy my suite mates were there and had someone come and fix it. I hoped the new day would bring joy.

Laurel was still sleeping. I didn't know too much about the girl that lay just a few feet away from me. She seemed nice, and I appreciated the fact that she had my back when it came to our new suite mates Jewels and Anna.

One thing I'd learned was that being black is hard and being a woman is hard. It's not that easy being a Christian either. Though I didn't know who Payton was, I knew who I was trying to be—and that was a good person. It was gonna be interesting with those two crazy girls, Jewels and Anna, on the other side of the bathroom, because I was only gonna take so much of their mess.

I've found that most of the time when you have something bad, you also have something good, and Laurel was a good white girl and a good roommate so far. She was a good Christian to whom I hoped I could grow closer.

My cousin Pillar was going to be a senior. I was so glad that we had resolved our issues. Being biracial is tough in this world. It gave my heart joy to know that in the end we had worked through the issues, and she knew I was only a phone call away. If she ever needed a friend, I would be there. Though she hadn't accepted Christ, she had accepted me with all my faults. Though she had some, too, being with her taught me that I can't judge people if I've got charges against me. I can't polish other folks if I'm tarnished. I can't try to fix others if I'm broken. For the first time, I realized I'm not "Perfect Payton."

Looking at the dawn of the new day, I thought of both of my ex-boyfriends a few hundred feet away in some other dorm as roommates. I thought of my parents miles away in the comfort of their own home. I then realized, with God being everywhere, I'd have help finding my way. I had to look forward to the future, and He's got a lot of good stuff for me. I've got to believe that I am somebody, and I'm gonna stand on God's Word no matter what comes my way.

Though I didn't get any sleep, I put on my slippers and thought, *I can't live in fear. I've gotta look toward the future with excitement and quit reliving the past . . . .*

2

Chasing Peers' Acceptance

Why are they staring at me? I said to myself as I ate lunch for the first time in the school cafeteria.

The food was OK, but it had nothing on Mom's home-cooked grub. As I looked up from eating the mushy mashed potatoes, I saw two girls checking me out. I had noticed them watching me about five minutes earlier. The first time, I thought they just simply glanced my way at the same time I glanced theirs. But then, more and more as I tried to play it off and act like I wasn't looking at them, I noticed them really staring at me. They were talking about me. I wasn't sure they were saying anything negative, but that was my guess. College was a trip.

One thing being a debutante did teach me last year was how to get along and appreciate everybody's differences. Accept people for who they are, that kind of thing. Make new friends and not be intimidated by qualities in others that I find attractive and I myself lack.

However, when two adorable African-American girls would

rather sit across the room and chatter about me than come over and introduce themselves, I knew that they didn't have the same privileges that I'd had. I didn't mean that arrogantly. You could have the best of the best and just be downright unfriendly. I think the village that raised me, that brought me out to society, taught me values that made my stock go up, and I appreciated that.

The question was how long was I gonna sit there and let them pick me apart. I was starting to get self-conscious. Was it my hair? I was wearing a straw set—you know, where the hair stylist wraps your hair around straws, sits you under the dryer and then pulls them out and you have little, bitty, mini curls. It was kind of poofy, but I knew that within the course of the week it would fall. With registration, orientation, and me getting involved in freshman activities, fooling with my hair would be the last thing I wanted to worry with. Or maybe they were saying something good about me. Yeah, right! I doubted it, but either way I was tired of the looks, and I had finished my meal, so I picked up my tray and headed to put it up.

I was behind them when I reentered the room. I heard the one with soft lemon skin and naturally wavy hair say, "Where'd she go?"

Then the milk-chocolate girl with short clothes and a sassy, short haircut said, "Probably to take off them ugly shoes she had on." Then they giggled.

"So what's wrong with my shoes?" I replied. "These Reebok Slides are very comfortable."

They looked so stunned. Yep, I had caught them, and they couldn't say, "Girl, we weren't talkin' 'bout you." If nothing else, black women have instincts. They know when another sistah is checking them out.

"Well, it might have seemed that we were being naughty, but we were simply making an observation," the prissy, light brown one said. "Don't take it the wrong way," she added.

I gave a fake smile. There was no right way to take someone saying something negative about you.

"I'm Blake Carrington from Atlanta, and this is Shanay. Tell her where you're from." She hit her on the arm.

"I'm sure she don't wanna know all dat," Shanay said.

They were cute but definitely weird. Earlier I would have thought I could have befriended them. However, after briefly talking with them, I didn't see any close friendships developing. They seemed quite stuck on themselves.

"See y'all around," I said as I threw up my hand.

"So do you want to go with me?" Laurel asked me in our room.

"No," I told her with disgust. "Going to a white frat party does not seem interesting. No!"

"Well, darn, Payton. You don't have to be so touchy. You don't want to hear me play my music . . . It bothers you. You don't wanna try out for a sorority with me. I'm trying, but you're not making it easy."

Laurel and I had roomed together for about four days. Though she was cool, she was still white, and we were not gonna be totally there with each other. I wanted her to like me, but I didn't wanna be fake. And I didn't wanna go to a stupid white party and be the only shot of pepper there. No, it just wasn't interesting to me, but who could blame me about the country music junk? It just wasn't my taste. Some pop music I liked, but country? That's pushing it too far. I'm well-rounded, but uh-uh, some of her stuff is not for me.

My mother is a Delta, and I didn't even know if I wanted to pledge that one day. But she would tell me I was stupid for talkin' 'bout whether I wanna be an Alpha Gam or a Tri Del. Me wanting to pledge a white sorority wouldn't be the only drawback. They probably wouldn't want me anyway. Laurel

24

was so sweet and naive that when I finally said no forcefully about some things, she got all sensitive.

"Look," I said, "I'm sorry you think I'm being abrupt, but there are just some things about black people that you have got to understand."

"I want to understand."

"Our suite mates don't even want to get to know me. Why do you care so much?" I asked with genuine concern. "We're cool. We don't have to be best friends."

With a sad tone she said, "Yeah, you're right. We can just exist. We don't really have to like it."

"I'm not saying that. Ugh!"

I went into the bathroom and slammed the door. She was such a baby! I'd heard white girls were soft. Being here for only a while had shown me that there was truth to that statement. But the girls on the other side of that door, however, were definitely tough ones. It was funny because Laurel wanted to get to know me so well, and they didn't want to have a thing to do with me. Could I just find a happy medium someplace?

As I brushed my teeth, I looked up in the mirror. The image staring back at me looked as it always looked. A confident, attractive young lady with a lot of potential and a smiling face. The only difference was this time after rinsing out my mouth, there was no genuine smile plastered there. I was baffled because I didn't really know whom to lean on. My girls Lynzi, Dymond, and Rain had been more than anchors over the last several years of my life—they were a part of me. We thought alike. Thought so much alike that sometimes we really got on one another's nerves. We enjoyed one another, and now they were not part of my daily life.

Though Dakari and Tad were somewhere on campus, the relationships I shared with them were strained. I thought it was gonna be easy to make other close black girlfriends. However, when I saw them on campus, freshmen like me since most of the upperclassmen hadn't arrived yet, they seemed more into what I was wearing than what I was about as a person. That's just not the kind of friends I wanted to make. I wanted to find something in common with my dear white roommate, whom I like, but not being on the same wavelength was tough.

"I miss my friends!" I said aloud.

Two years ago, I'd read a book for class called *Who Moved My Cheese?* Although I thought the title was stupid, after getting into the book I grew to like it. It was about two mice and two humans being in a maze and trying to find the quickest way to the cheese. Basically, what I learned from reading the book was that mice don't really think too much about change. If the cheese is moved in the maze, they just go and sniff it out, no big deal. But for humans, they get so comfortable with where the cheese is that if it is moved, it's almost as if life is over. We as humans need to think more like mice and not get so stressed out every time our cheese is moved. Especially me, Payton Skky.

Well, as far as friends in my life, the cheese was definitely moved, and I was not happy about it at all. I could think like the humans in the book and really stress out and be in such a pity party that my whole freshman year goes by and life is just horrible. Or I could think like the mice and find someone to fill the girlfriend thing in my life.

So I said to myself in the mirror, "OK, I'm going to think like the mice."

I opened the door and called out to Laurel. "Do you have any plans for dinner?"

"No, no, I don't. I've got to do sorority stuff next week, and I'll probably be gone most of the time, so you won't have to worry about listening to my country music because I won't be here."

"You know, I'm sorry about that," I said to her. "I'm not sorry about not liking country music because I don't, but you like it. I can stand to listen to it sometimes, I guess. You should be comfortable in your own room."

After telling Laurel I was sorry for being mean to her and truly letting her know why, she said she understood. My mood could have been because it was just that time of the month. I realized another reason why I had been so cranky. Being in hot Georgia, with a cramping stomach and no friends, could make me a crabby girl.

The two of us went over to the cafeteria. I hadn't eaten there since earlier in the week when I had encountered Blake and Shanay. The food tasted better, maybe because I had a new attitude. I was determined to find the good in stuff rather than point out the negatives. It still wasn't Mom's food, but it was better than all the fast food I had been stuffing my belly with over the last couple of days.

Laurel and I started talking about things that we have in common. The one big thing that we shared was the fact that we both had ex-guys at this school. Though she didn't have two ex-boyfriends like me, the one that she did have sounded like an interesting character. When she told me their story of how he was so mean to her after their breakup, I wanted to punch him out. I didn't know him, but what a jerk! Maybe it was more of my hormones than anything, but based on the profile she had painted of him, I didn't like him.

"Excuse me, ladies," a warm, authoritative voice spoke. "My name is Karlton Kincaid, and I just wanna snag a minute of this pretty lady's time," he said as he looked at Laurel, but touched my shoulder.

"Sure," Laurel said. "I need more ketchup for my fries anyway." She got up and left.

He sat down beside me and told me all about himself. This Tampa native was now a junior at Georgia. He invited me to a party that was sponsored by the Student Government Association for the black freshmen. When he said he was the director of minority recruitment, I started to holler.

"Wow! Well, did you know Hayli?"

I asked him that because she was Dakari's brother's fiancée, and she had held that position last year. She basically got me to come here. When we talked, he told me that he was very good friends with Hayli and that she had told him to look out for Payton Skky. He was happy he'd run into me before school had started.

He wore glasses and had on a bow tie, which on another day I might have found quite nerdy, but today I found it had appeal. He had a unique sense of style. He was very refined, kind of like a white boy in black skin. I was digging it.

"You're cuter than she said you were," he commented, flattering me.

"Well, she didn't tell me about you at all, and when I talk to her I'm gonna have to ask her why she was holdin' out," I joked back.

He blushed. "Do you have plans for this evening?"

"No. My roommate is going to a KA party, and I don't think I'll be joining her, so I thought my night was going to be dead. I haven't heard anything about this party."

"Well, we're just tryin' to throw something together. When I bumped into a lot of new freshmen, they had been saying that they hadn't had a chance to meet one another. Quite a few black students enrolled. We've got about three hundred and something."

"Really? I haven't seen that many around here."

He said, "Yeah, so we're throwin' a little somethin' together. It's not on campus, so hopefully people will be able to find it. But my past experience tells me that we can always find a party."

"Yeah," I said, laughing back.

"And I've been on campus all week, and I have not bumped into you," he said.

"Well, I've been here. I've been around. What time does the party start?"

"We'll kick off around nine, but you know it won't be jumpin' 'til about eleven."

"Cool. Thanks for inviting me."

"Well, you'll have to save me a dance."

"I'll have to do that." I smiled as he got up from his seat. "Bye, Karlton Kincaid."

As I watched him walk away, I felt more relaxed. I was worried about just making new friends, like Blake and Shanay. They were obviously not the only ones I had to choose from. I was looking forward to the party later that evening. Hopefully it would prove to be exciting for me. It was quite interesting as I watched the tall, slim guy stroll farther and farther out of my presence. It was a brief encounter but definitely one that was intriguing and memorable.

"Thanks for picking us up," Dakari said as he and Tad got into my ride.

They both had cars, but the football coach did not want freshmen ballplayers to have access to them during camp, so they called me and asked if I was going to the party. Chauffeuring my two ex-boyfriends around was going to be interesting.

They had been together as roommates for a week. Day in and day out at training camp and all that was affiliated with that. They had the pressure of learning the plays and winning the coach's favor. But just watching them walk to my car, I could see a bond was forming, which was quite weird because the two of them had despised each other in high school. They were both great running backs, and now they were friends. Well, maybe "friends" was too strong a word.

I couldn't help but say, "This is a trip, the two of y'all tight. This is real crazy."

"Who said we were tight?" Tad said as he settled into the backseat.

"For real. Dang, it ain't like that," Dakari said as he tried kissing me on the cheek.

"Don't even go there. You know you wrong!" I said as I shoved him in the side.

"We're goin' to a party! Hands up! Hands up!" Dakari joked.

"You better act like you got some sense. Don't be givin' my school a bad name."

"Yo' skirt kind of short," Dakari said. "Look, Tad."

Tad peeped over my shoulder and said, "Yeah, I see what you mean. What's up wit' dat, Payton?"

"It's only 'cause I'm driving. My skirt is not short. Ain't nobody talkin' 'bout what y'all got on."

To think I worried about how we were going to get along. The three of us had a fun relationship. I didn't belong to either one of those guys. They clearly understood that, and so did I. Yet we had so much history that there was no way we could not be there for one another. So it was kind of like I had big brothers at school with me. Only by a couple of months, but they were lookin' out for me nonetheless. I'm sure there was a little bit more going on underneath that, too, but for the moment we put all that aside and were just buds. I was cool with my new role as I escorted them to the party.

Unfortunately, two hours into it when the place got packed and I was standing there with these two gorgeous guys on both sides of me, I got a lot of mean looks from a lot of sistahs. No guys were coming up to me asking me to dance, and that wasn't cool.

"OK, y'all go y'all's way. I will let you guys know when it's time to go."

"Oooohh. Don't let us miss curfew for real, for real," Dakari said.

Tad agreed, "Yeah. We gotta be back right at twelve. So it's eleven now, and it is not our fault folks waited to come, but we gotta go in a little while."

"That's cool. I don't wanna be out all night anyway," I told them. "Now, y'all go. Leave me alone so I can make some friends. Get my groove on and dance."

"You better be good," Dakari said to me.

Dakari being the clown he was, headed over to the dance floor alone and started cutting up. Immediately, everybody checked him out and knew that he was going to be one of those guys everybody wanted to know. He was a nut. I hadn't seen that side of him since eleventh grade.

Tad, on the other hand, was kind of reserved and stood by me a second and said, "So how've you been? We haven't talked in a week. What's been up with you? You missed me or what?" he whispered.

"You missed me?" I asked him as he looked one way and I looked the other. It was so funny because we were acting like we weren't together. However, the stuff we were talking about was together stuff.

"I thought about you when I was out in the hot sun and didn't want to run another lap and needed a pretty sight to keep me going."

"Yeah, I thought about you. I've been praying for you and your camp. I've been praying for you and Dakari, hoping you wouldn't kill each other in that room. I guess it's kind of been a prayer answered."

"Yeah, we're gettin' along. He's cool. We're gonna be OK . . . I guess."

"Great," I replied.

Dakari came back over and grabbed Tad. "Come on, man. Let's dance with the honeys."

They went cruising and checking out all the girls on the

31

scene. Though Tad was a strong Christian, he was still a guy.

This is gonna be hard, I thought: *My two men checkin' out other girls.*

I looked over and saw Blake and Shanay walk in.

"Dannnng!" I heard Dakari yell as he hit Tad on the back.

I couldn't even stand it, so I walked to the rest room. When I came out, Tad was dancing with Blake, and Dakari was dancing with Shanay. My head was hurting.

"You lookin' at the dance floor mighty hard, lady," I heard someone from behind me say.

"Karlton! Hey!" I said as I turned around, happy to see him.

"You savin' a dance for me?"

"Sure, why not?"

I grabbed his hand and ushered him between Tad and Dakari. I was determined that they would see me having more fun than them. As I danced, I grabbed my waistband and rolled up my skirt an inch or two. The guys talked about it being short in the car, but it was really short now. I don't know what I was thinking; I just wanted their eyes to be on me and not on those chicks they were dancing with. Yes, I had issues, but it's what I did. In my heart, I was convinced that I shouldn't try to lure a guy by being sexy. What a shallow relationship that would be.

"You can really move," Karlton said to me as though he was into me, too.

"You ain't as stiff as you look," I said to him.

When the slow song came on, Karlton automatically assumed we were going to dance together. He grabbed my waist and pulled me to him. We rocked to the left, went to the right, skipped a beat, and then rocked back to the other side. He had rhythm. As we circled around, I saw both Tad and Dakari rocking, too.

"So, can I get your number and call you?" Karlton asked.

"Yeah, sure."

"Are you OK, Payton? You don't seem to be all into this dance," he said as I stepped on his foot.

"Yeah, I'm sorry. What'd you say?" I asked him, clearly out of it.

I looked down at my watch, and it was now eleven-thirty. As close as we were, packed up in the little place, I could read Blake and Shanay's lips. They were digging my guys a little too much.

I pushed Karlton back and said to Dakari and Tad, "Y'all, it's time to go."

"It's time to go? Who are you talkin' to?" Blake said.

"I'm talkin' to him, and I'm talkin' to him," I uttered, pointing to Tad and Dakari.

"Dang! It's that time already?" Dakari said.

"Yep. Gotta go."

At that moment the guys were clueless to the women, who were shocked that I was commanding such attention. I knew exactly what I was doing.

"See y'all later. We gotta go," Dakari said to the girls.

Blake and Shanay stood on the dance floor alone with their arms crossed. They were rolling their eyes at me. I had wanted so much to be accepted by those girls when I saw them, days back. Then they started talking about me like I didn't have it goin' on. Well now, the two men that they were into were riding with me, and I for sure had it going on.

"Don't pout, ladies. It doesn't look pleasin'," I teased as I walked past them. "I saw y'all were into my men. Don't worry; they are taken. They both want me. I just haven't decided which one I want."

"You know those guys for real?" Blake asked.

Tainting the truth, I said, "Boyfriends. They like my shoes."

As I walked away from them with my head upright, I felt good. Maybe too good. I knew I was cocky and didn't

necessarily have to be, but all week I had been trying to figure out where I belonged.

At that moment, I knew I could find my way. Whether
they'd admit it or not, I had Blake and Shanay's respect. As
far as getting along with my roommate, I knew I could do
some things with Laurel. Where Tad and Dakari were concerned, I knew we were still figuring all that out. Fitting in
didn't have to be such a burden anymore. I could just let it
all go, be me, and quit chasing peers' acceptance.

3

Wanting to Control

As I hit the button for both Dakari and Tad to get in, I had a mean look on my face. I was quite angry at them. Dancing all up on them girls. It really was getting under my skin. Maybe I should call myself out and say that I was pouting, because that's what I was doing.

"Y'all better hurry up and get in," I said.

"What's wrong with you?" Tad asked, detecting that I had some sort of problem.

Before I could say anything about their dancing, Dakari busted me. "So who was the nerd you were on the floor with? He had his hands all over you, didn't he? Dannng!"

"Like you can talk!" I said to him quickly. "And his hands were not all over me."

Brothas trip me out. They think they can dance all crazy, but let a sistah try to do it, something's wrong with her. But deep inside I was happy he noticed. Tad was quiet.

"The two of y'all were dancin' worse than me. Plus, y'all don't even know those girls. You guys need to watch out.

You play football for Georgia, too! Don't be stupid. They were trying to latch on to you guys just because y'all are on the team."

"What are you talking about, Payton? We were just dancin'," Tad said from the back.

"Come on, man. I'm sure you know what she's talkin' 'bout. You thought you had girls at your high school wantin' you, but playin' on this level it's nothin' but a sure thang. My brother said he got them digits all the time. He had a steady girl, and that just helped because women love it when they got to take it from somebody else."

"Ugh! You make me sick," I said, hitting Dakari in the chest. "Drake is a jerk, and so are you."

"I'm just being real. Don't get mad because I'm tellin' the truth. If we're gonna be friends, then you need to know how I think."

"I was your girl. I know how you think. That's what bothers me, because I already know how you think. It just makes my skin crawl."

"Pull over at McDonald's and let me get a quick bite," Dakari said, ignoring my earlier statement.

"Look at that drive-thru line," I said to him. "You're gonna miss curfew."

"I'll run in right quick."

I swooped in the McDonald's, and Dakari jumped out.

"I'll hook y'all up," he said to Tad and me.

Before I could say anything, Tad asked me, "So who's the bean-pie guy?"

"What?" I said, laughing.

"Don't trip. The bean-pie guy. The man that looks like the guy on the corner selling bean pies and passing out literature."

"Oh, see, you are wrong for that," I told him. "That guy is so smart. He's in SGA and really nice. His name is Karlton."

"Oh, he's really nice? You'd better watch yourself, Payton.

Short skirts, dancin' close. You don't have to wonder—I was jealous." Tad leaned over the front of the car seat.

Though Dakari was still my boy, and I cared for him deeply, I could tell the difference. Dakari's feelings for me didn't go as deep as Tad's. Tad thought of me the same way I thought of him, but we agreed not to entertain those feelings. Truth be told, I wanted to control both Dakari and Tad. I hoped they both would be after me. I don't know why, but when I really looked at myself, that was what was there.

When Tad didn't get the response he wanted from me, he leaned back in the seat. I could tell he was irritated, but, shoot, I didn't know what to say. Deep down, I wanted him to hug me and hold me, but that would only lead to trouble.

"So how's football stuff?" I asked, just trying to make conversation.

I hated dead air. The silence, no words; it was not what the two of us used to have. So I had to say something.

However, he quickly reminded me I had said that already. "You asked me earlier about football stuff. Nothing's changed since then."

"Why are you getting so touchy with me?"

"Because you don't like me dancin' with other people, and I don't like you dancin' with other people. Yet, we're not gonna do anything about it. We're just gonna be friends. You know, Payton, I just don't know."

"What don't you know? It can't be the way that I want it. Plus, the way you were today, all into that girl, you are fixin' to get over me just like Dakari has."

"This isn't about Dakari. I was just dancin'. Don't confuse me with him. If you think about it, I know you know my true heart and my real feelings for you. So much has happened between us that I don't know what it was that broke us up. But I'm gonna ask you right here and now.

Since you trippin' about other people and I'm trippin' about other people, is that the way you want it, Payton?"

I tossed the question around in my mind a thousand times after he asked it. All I had to say was, "I wanna be with you," and cast aside my pride. Stupidly, my tongue just wouldn't say a thing.

All of a sudden, Dakari opened the door and saved me from having to speak, "What's up! Y'all looking kind of serious in here. Have some fries."

"Where have you been, stranger?" I said to Laurel as she tiptoed into the room, trying not to wake me. "You can turn on the light; I'm up."

Laurel whispered, trying to avoid me, "Payton, I'm so tired. It's been such a long day."

"Really, tell me about it. Did you get the sorority you wanted or what? How'd it all go?" I asked, wanting to know.

She went on to tell me that during the rush period with white sororities, girls go to different sorority houses and introduce themselves. After that initial visit, the candidates then write on a card their top three choices in order, and at the same time the sorority sisters meet after they had these potential pledges come through. The sororities list the girls that they wanted. The lists were then matched up, and to make a long story short, most girls don't get their first choice.

"So when will you know?" I asked her.

"Not until tomorrow, and I wish I could just pick Alpha Gam and that was the way it was going to be."

"So please tell me that our suite mates were wrong and having me as a roommate didn't lower your chances."

"They never asked me about my roommate, so no. You didn't have a negative effect on the outcome. If I don't get in, it will strictly be on me."

"I'll be there for you," I said to her genuinely. "If you don't get in, you don't need to be there. They seem like a bunch of stuck-up white girls, if you ask me. Why would you want to be in it anyway? I've never seen any of them, but I've surely heard about them."

"Payton, we are not a bunch of stuck-up white girls! Sororities do community service. Just being able to enjoy my college years was the main reason for joining. If you're gonna go to UGA, it's cool to affiliate with a sorority."

"Really?"

"Yeah, there are formal dances. Each sorority has a brother fraternity that works with them. So in an instant, you get to work with nice guys."

"Yeah, right. They do a lot of hazing and drinking beer from what I've heard."

"At least they don't get beat up, Payton," Laurel said, putting me in my place.

I questioned. "What do you know about black Greeks?"

"More than you know about white Greeks. We'll talk about it sometime. There's more to me than you think."

"OK, Laurel, just don't get taken for granted. You will be at one of those formals, and somebody will slip something in your drink. Don't be naive," I preached.

"Yeah, I'm aware of that, but I am saying that if I get into the right sorority, the fraternity they hook up with will be more valiant than one that's just about kegs of beer."

"Well, seems like you've thought it out, and you are doing good in the process. What happens if you don't get your top three?"

"I don't even want to think about it," she said as she got ready for bed.

"Well, being a gymnast should help, right?"

I was so excited that my roommate was on the gymnastics team. She wasn't like the top girls on scholarship, which is why she didn't have to live in their housing quarters. She was on the practice squad and that was phenomenal. The Lady Bulldogs have won many gymnastics championships.

"I just think I am better than two of the freshmen on scholarship. I've seen them working in the gym. On the vault, I'm so much better than they are, it's ridiculous. Not only on vault, but floor, beam, and the uneven bars. One girl fell twice today. The coach just really likes them. It seems like she is giving me such a hard time."

"Laurel, what are you talking about?" I was almost asleep at that time.

"Nothing. It's just my problems. Not that I expect you to listen."

"Not that I don't want to listen—I just don't understand gymnastics. You made the squad, and two girls fell. I don't understand that stuff. It sounds to me that maybe if you continue to work hard and practice you can create a spot on the travel team. When does the season start?"

"January."

"There you go, girl. You have a whole semester. You never know what will happen between now and then."

"Yeah, but it's just unfair. I should not have to work so hard to be on the team. I should automatically be able to be on it. It's not right."

"Life's not fair. Welcome to the real world."

"Why are you so cold? What's happened to you to make you so bitter with the world?"

"Why does everybody think I'm so bitter? My ex-boyfriend thought I was bitter yesterday. I just don't get it. Did you go to freshmen orientation?" I asked, trying to change the subject. "Did you meet any interesting people?"

"Between gymnastics, pledging the sorority, and dealing with my jerk ex-boyfriend, I don't have time or energy to meet any interesting people."

"Now who's being crabby?" I asked.

"Maybe we should just go to sleep and talk tomorrow."

"Yeah, maybe we should."

We both have issues, I thought as I tried desperately to fall asleep. It was hard to befriend anybody when you weren't happy with yourself. I think that was probably my main problem, but maybe I just didn't want to admit it at the time. I had boy problems; she had boy problems. I had girl problems; she had girl problems. Just issues. We were about to start our freshman year, and our minds were far from clear. It would be a miracle if we learned anything with our present mind-set. Something was going to have to change us, but I had no clue what that something was going to be.

A few minutes later as I started to drift off, I heard sobs. I thought I was imagining it because I was so tired. I tried listening more intensely, and, sure enough, it was Laurel.

"What's wrong?" I asked her.

"You just do not know. I feel so picked on by the gymnastics team. It's like the other girls think that I'm nothing. The coach hates me. I just hate my life right now. Sometimes I am so tempted to just quit and go home."

I didn't know what to say. I didn't know what to do. I wasn't very happy with my life either. Giving any words of wisdom would have been like the blind leading the blind, so I couldn't give any words of comfort.

Lord, I thought, *I want things to be right. Right now they are just so wrong. This girl is over there crying, and I don't know what to do. I feel like crying, but I'm too tough at the moment to let out a tear. Help us. Help me and help her.*

All of a sudden, I got out of my bed and went over to her. I lifted her gently and placed her brunette hair in my bosom. I didn't say anything, and she didn't say anything. I was just simply there for her to hold her and let her know that though I couldn't make it better, I shared her burden. Hopefully, when we embraced, she got the subliminal meaning that this was just part time, and in the end all the pain would pass.

I wondered how my girls were doing. I knew I couldn't call D.C.—my mom had told me to keep the bill down. However, an Atlanta phone call wouldn't cost too much money. I received a letter from Rain, my girlfriend at Spelman. She had given me her new number, so I wanted to check in on her.

I pulled the phone into the bathroom so as not to disturb Laurel, who had finally drifted to sleep. I think her tears made her tired. I was glad she was able to rest.

"Raaain! It's me, if you're there, pick up!" I whispered loudly into her machine.

When I was about to hang up, she picked up the phone, and I was so thankful because I really needed to talk to her.

After I told her mostly everything she said, "Daaang, Payton. Girrrl, drama just follows you, don't it?"

"Well, how 'bout you. How are things at the AUC?"

"Girl, Atlanta University Center got it goin' on. It is so much fun here. My roommate is nice. She's from New York."

"New York?"

"Yes, New York. She is so cool. Her name is Kiana Gresham, and we've got so much in common. We both are psych majors; she played basketball, too, though neither of us is gonna play in college. She's cool. I've been making a lot of other friends, too. They're pretty nice. People used to tell me that Spelman was gonna be a lot of competition. There'll be some of that, but for the most part we are probably a unified freshman class."

"I'm jealous," I uttered in honesty.

"See, why you gotta playa hate?"

"'Cause it's not like that for me. My roommate and I don't bond. I guess I shouldn't say that. I just had her head in my lap."

"What?"

"She was crying. Girl, she's got issues."

"Well, it sounds like you do, too. I'll be praying for you. Look, I'm headed out to a party."

"What, girl? We had one last night."

"Really?"

"Yeah, you'll never guess who I went with."

"Who?"

"Dakari *and* Tad."

"You lyin'!"

"Girl, I'm serious."

"I sure would have loved to have been there. Girl, who did you dance with?"

"Neither one. I met this guy who's a junior here. He's totally different from the guys we like, but he's got quite a style. I danced with him."

"But you went with Dakari and Tad? OK, I'm confused. We'll have to pick this up another time, 'cause I have to go. Girl, hang in there and be excited. It'll get better, and you can come visit me soon."

"Yeah, OK, Miss Too Good to Talk to Your Friend."

"Oh, no. Don't do me like that, Payton," Rain said.

"Shoot, I'm just playin'. Go have a good time and have one for me while you're at it."

"Girl, you know I will. 'Bye."

" 'Bye."

Just as I put the phone down, it rang. I thought it was a back ring from Rain, but it wasn't. Surprisingly it was Tad.

"What are you doing up so late?" I asked.

"Well, we haven't had time to talk since yesterday when your boy came back, and I just wanted to see if you had any thoughts or an answer to the question I asked last night."

"I don't know what's best. I thought about you today, that's for sure. I'm not even happy with me right now."

"What do you mean you're not happy with you?"

43

"I don't know. I miss my friends. I miss home. I wouldn't be any good as a girlfriend. I'm self-conscious with everything I put on because of girls telling me my shoes are ugly. I'm not together like I was a year ago. I probably wasn't even together then because if I was I would not be this untogether now."

"OK, slow down. You are not making any sense."

"I know I'm not, but I guess I'm saying this to be fair to you. I know I need you in my life right now."

"Sounds like you need Christ in your life."

"Yeah, maybe I do. I've been here a week, and all I've done is pray. I haven't picked up the Bible or anything. Maybe that's what I need. So are you playin' tomorrow?"

"No, that's why I'm callin' you. I'm not in the rotation. I'm not even on special teams."

"You're not injured or anything, are you?"

"No, I'm just not playing. I'll be on the sidelines, but that's just about it. Your boy will be suitin' up, though."

"What? Really?"

I didn't want to say it, but I thought that Tad was before Dakari in the rotation. I guess something happened to change all that, and I didn't want to go there. If Tad wanted to talk about it, he'd offer the information. Since he didn't, I didn't want to push.

"I know I played good enough to be on that doggone field tomorrow. I just lost my temper with the coach, and I guess this is his way of punishing me. I'm supposed to be out there on that field. Dang!"

"I'm not up on football, and I was talking about the same thing with my roommate."

"Your roommate?"

"Yeah, we talk now. She's on the gymnastics team, and she's not in the rotation or the travel squad, or something's not going right. Georgia and their sports are starting to give me a headache. Well, anyway, I didn't know much about it, but I tried to give her advice. The counsel I gave was to work hard, and before you know it, your stuff will be turned around, and you'll be on the field."

"Easier said than done, Payton. You don't understand."

"I know you're a good ballplayer. I understand that. The coach won't be able to keep your talent down for long. Keep working at it, and use that frustration for fuel to get you where you want to be. You're gonna be the main man," I said, laughing. "You're gonna be in charge, watch."

He started laughing, "Thanks for talking to me. You got tickets for tomorrow?"

"Yeah."

"My family is gonna eat with the Grahams," he told me.

"Wow, I didn't realize they were coming up."

"Yeah, you wanna come with us?" Tad offered.

"Sure, it's not like I have anything else goin' on."

"Oh, so what are you trying to say?"

"It's still kind of weird with me hanging with you and Dakari. Now y'all are going to bring your families together. Dang, what are you trying to do to me?"

"Well, you know my mom would love to see you. Since her son ain't gonna be playin', she's gonna need some reason to come up here."

"She's not payin' for school, so you know she's happy."

"Yeah, well, I'll see you after the game. Good night."

"Good night."

———

"Hi, Payton. Anybody sitting with you?" Blake and Shanay asked me at the cafeteria that next morning.

I looked at them very strangely. Weren't these the same two girls who so recently talked about me? Now they were asking to sit with me. What in the world was up with that?

Because I was intrigued enough to find out what they

wanted, I said, "Sure, have a seat."

Blake started, "Well, Payton."

"How'd you know my name?" I asked her.

"Everybody knows your name. Plus, I think you said it when we met. We just wanted to come over and apologize to you because we obviously got off on the wrong foot. There are not enough sistahs here for us to be trippin' like we did."

"What? You mean talkin' about my shoes and everything?"

"Yeah, something like that."

"Something like that? Y'all need to admit y'all were talking about me. It was high schoolish."

"Yeah, well everybody makes mistakes," Shanay said. "We just wanted to call a truce so we can start over. You're a cute girl. Not to say that we were intimidated, but . . . " She looked at Blake, and both admitted they were intimidated.

"By me?"

They just didn't know how much I was struggling within. They were the cute ones. I felt I didn't measure up. So it was somewhat comforting to hear that they thought the same of me.

"It's only a few of us, and we need to stick together, not tear one another down," I said.

"We couldn't agree more. So are you going to the game today?" they asked.

"Yeah."

Shanay said nicely, "You going with a roommate or anybody in particular, because we're going. We'd love for you to hang with us."

I hadn't had true sistah time since I had gotten here. I had the one run-in at the dorm with the girl Cammie, but I hadn't seen her since. Not that I had been looking for her, either. Hanging out with Blake and Shanay might be fun.

We laughed and cut up at the game. It was as if we had never had any bad blood between us. They were pretty cool.

I found out that Blake is the mayor's daughter. Talk about big time. I see why she had a little chip on her shoulder. She was used to being ushered around in limos for the past couple of years of her life.

Shanay, on the other hand, came from modest means. She went to South West Dekalb High School, one of the premier black high schools in the Atlanta area. Being in a tough black school and being one of the hottest girls, I understood her a little more, too.

I was once described as an open blossom, as opposed to an onion peeler. Meaning that when I meet people, my life is an open book. I tell too much sometimes. I'm overly friendly. As opposed to an onion peeler, who just reveals one layer at a time. Those people don't tell too much until it's time to reveal the next thing.

With these girls I gave them the true 411 on Dakari, Tad, and myself. The crazy triangle. They wanted to know if I was really serious the other night when I said those were my guys, and I was all too eager to tell them what I meant. One might have been the mayor's daughter, and one might have had the finest body I had ever seen, but at that moment I had something they wish they had—dibs on two gorgeous guys. The two hottest freshmen in our small world basically belonged to me.

"But right now, you don't go with either of them?" Blake asked for clarification.

"That's true."

Shanay cut in. "So you gotta hook us up."

"Wait—what part of my story did you not hear?"

"You can't have both of 'em," Shanay said.

"Well, let me figure out which one I want before you try to take one of them."

"Maybe if you can't decide, then they'll make a decision for you," Blake replied.

"What are you tryin' to say?"

"I'm sayin'," Shanay said directly, "you can't have it both ways. There's no way you can want them and not want anybody else to like them. They're guys, and if we're not the sistahs that are gonna take them, you better believe there is gonna be some other girls that want them. You got good taste, and I went to school with some fine brothas at South West, and they ain't got nothin' on them brothas that you said were yours. Oh, yes, I want some of that, and I'm just letting you know."

The fun was starting to fade. Dakari was on the field in special teams and ran a kickoff return ninety-nine yards. It was an exhilarating moment. I was so proud that he was my boy. I quickly thought about Tad and saw him on the sideline. I knew that, because he was a Christian, in his heart he'd be equally ecstatic for Dakari. However, the human side of him would be slightly dejected.

"So what are you doing after the game?" the girls asked me as we noticed only two minutes on the clock.

I was going to have them come with me to dinner; however, when they said they were after these guys, I didn't know what I was thinking. They only wanted to be friends with me to get close to Dakari and Tad, and I wasn't going to help. Yeah, they would probably find a way to get Dakari and Tad on their own, but they weren't going to use me as easy bait.

"With a score like this, winning by twenty something points, I'm sure the ballplayers are gonna have something tonight," Shanay probed.

"Maybe I'll catch y'all there. I'm gonna meet with some friends."

"The guys?" Shanay picked some more.

"Oh, see why you gotta be all in my business?" I teased but really meant it. "No, some old but new friends."

"You know she wouldn't do her girls like that," Blake said. "If she was meeting the guys, she would take us with her. Right, Payton?"

"You know it," I said back to her.

We were eating at Piccadilly's, and I had such a good time with my former beaux' mothers. Mrs. Graham and Mrs. Taylor were so sweet. Two totally different women, but they were both my friends. They never even mentioned the fact that I was no longer with their sons. They just said they were glad I was in their sons' lives, and they wished me the best at UGA. Mr. Graham said he hoped I went to see some of Drake's games with the Falcons.

Everybody was praising Dakari about the run he had earlier. When I went to give him a big hug, he kissed me on the lips in front of everybody. I didn't know where Tad was, but I know he saw it. Though I liked the kiss, I didn't like that Dakari manipulated to get it and basically tried to showboat. When Dakari released me, I looked around for Tad; he was nowhere to be found.

Everybody wanted it their way, including me. I wanted to write my own destiny, but as Tad had pointed out the night before, God was nowhere in the picture. I was not desiring the Almighty to lead my steps. Payton Skky knew what was best for her, and unfortunately her way wasn't working out. In the midst of me not getting my way, I was becoming dishonest, jealous, bitter, and just all the things that weren't of God.

I enjoyed Dakari's kiss because he was the star of the day, and I wanted to be with a winner. As he planted his lips on mine, I thought about Shanay, who desperately wished she could be with him, and yet he was kissing me. How small-minded that was, but that was the mind I possessed at the time.

I had to get hold of myself. I knew I had to change my ways. If I was going to succeed in life, it wasn't going to be because of my own design. It had to be because I surrendered my life to the Lord and allowed His plan for my life to be the plan. In order to have these things go right, I had to release the desire of wanting to control.

4

Experiencing
New Emotions

"So what kind of day is it gonna be, pumkin?"

"A great day, Daddy . . . a great day," I said into the receiver.

He had called early that morning to encourage me and get me excited about my first day of college. I remember on my first day of kindergarten that I was so nervous. I didn't want to go. Daddy had put me on top of the bathroom sink in my parents' bathroom, and I got to help him shave.

He said, "You know what? It's gonna be a great day today, Payton. Can you say, 'Great day, Daddy'?"

I replied with zest, "Hmmmmm, it's gonna be a great day!"

Through that I got encouraged. In fact, I grew up saying, "It's gonna be a great day!" Sometime in high school, I thought it was stupid and moved away from the positive thinking. Daddy always told me that whatever you put in your mind is what's gonna come out. I was glad to hear him pump me up, because I was nervous. Really, really nervous.

"Well, your mom sends her love."

"Tell her I love her, too," I responded.

"Your brother started school last week. Now he's a junior, so he thinks he's the big cheese around there."

"Yeah, and he's got a car, too. Perry is big time," I joked. "I miss you guys, Dad."

"I know you do, baby. But now it's your turn to be a young woman. Remember, you just pick up that phone and call me if you need to talk."

"Yeah, I will. 'Bye, Dad. Sell some cars for me."

"There you go reading my mind. I'll do it. 'Bye."

During my senior year, my dad and I really didn't get a chance to talk. He was into increasing sales at the automobile dealership, and I was so busy being a senior that our friendship kind of took a backseat. But over the years, we were always tight. We were tighter than my mom and I were. Not that it was a bad thing—we were just tight. He always called me his first good bullet. So silly, but I was definitely Daddy's little girl.

It was good that he remembered my first day, and that my family wanted to wish me well. I knew that I couldn't screw up this chance. I'd always been a good student, and I wanted to make sure that I continued that. I wasn't just representing me alone, but my whole family was here with me. I had the responsibility of maintaining my family name.

"What should I wear?" Laurel asked as she came out of the bathroom.

"I'm not puttin' on nothin' special. I'm just going to class."

"You don't understand."

I understood, all right. There were gonna be tons of people in our classes. First impressions are always the most important. However, I wasn't sure if I'd see one black face all day long, so who cared what I had on? For Laurel, I could understand her dilemma: Chicks talking about one another. The same drama I faced with Blake and Shanay, but just on a much broader scale because it was gonna be way more of them.

"Maybe we should have gone to church yesterday," Laurel said to me.

We both were so exhausted that we had slept most of the day.

"We prayed. Ain't nothin' we can do about it now. Look, just go put on somethin' cute. Girl, you'll be fine. We'll go to church next week," I told her.

I still didn't understand why Laurel wasn't as happy as she could be. Yeah, sure, Branson, her ex-high-school love, was still on her mind, but she had gotten selected for the sorority of her choice. She was an Alpha Gamma Delta, and so was Jewels. Anna, on the other hand, didn't get into any of her three choices. I wasn't sure which one she ended up in, but supposedly it wasn't a real reputable one.

Jewels, trying to be all sly, approached Laurel on the side and asked Laurel to room with her and put Anna and me in a room together. Laurel declined, but I couldn't believe Jewels would have the gall to do that. Now that Anna wasn't in Jewels's sorority, she wasn't good enough to stay in her room. It was crazy to me. I was glad to hear that Laurel felt the same way, but I think that angered Jewels. She was not used to getting no for an answer. I steered clear of the chick because I didn't want to have to hurt her. I could sense that she was an absolute brat. A girl with a lot of brains, but she played the dumb role because she thought it would get her farther. Oh, she was slick, real slick.

I was already dressed in a T-shirt and jeans. I went to the bathroom to put makeup on. Also I had to brush my teeth.

When I opened the door Jewels screamed, "Can't you knock! Dang, Payton!"

"Can't you lock the door! If you don't want nobody to

come in, Jewels, you need to lock the door."

"I'll tell you when I'm done," she snapped back at me.

"Hurry up, Jewels. I have a nine o'clock class."

"You can't rush beauty. Tell her, Anna. Oh, you wouldn't know anything about that, now would you, dear?"

I slammed the door. I could not believe she had played that girl like that. Just because she got accepted by a group that the whole school deems as "it," she now is going to think she is "it" and is going to look at everyone as a notch below her level. Everyone but Laurel. She was trying to make Laurel into her new best friend. She must have popped into our room a thousand times the day before. "Laurel, do you want to go here? Laurel, do you want to go there? Laurel, what do you think of this dress?" I had to get up and lock her out because I got tired of seeing her fake smile intruding into my space.

While I was waiting on the bathroom, I got on my knees and prayed silently. *Lord, make today special. I got knots in my stomach; take them away. I pray for all of the students You had me meet, especially Laurel. She seems to be a little jittery, too. Let the teachers be nice and somewhat easy. Let me understand their method of teaching and keep my mind focused on the task at hand. Oh, yeah, and I pray for Tad and Dakari. Be with them, too. I love You, and I thank You. In Jesus' name. Amen.*

"Laurel, tell your roommate she can go to the bathroom now," I heard Jewels whisper to Laurel as if I were deaf.

I just simply got off my knees, walked past her, and went to the bathroom. I had to finish getting ready. Childish drama wasn't going to upset my morning.

I held my breath as I went up the stairs in the building for my first class. I was trying to find Room 228, Psychology 101.

"Hi, Payton," I heard a pleasant voice say.

When I looked up I saw Cammie. I hadn't seen her in the last couple of days, even though we lived in the same dorm. I guess we'd both been busy settling in.

"Hey, girl. What class are you goin' to?" I asked.

"Psychology."

"Really? I am, too. What room?"

"Two-twenty-eight."

"Oh, we're in the same class. Girl, I thought I was going to be the lone black."

"Me too," she said with honesty.

We hugged and walked around the corner.

Our teacher was a strong, tall Irish man, Mr. O'Conner. The pace was definitely faster than the one I was used to back at Lucy Laney. But thanks to Cammie, I could keep up.

"During this year," Mr. O'Conner said, "we are going to be concentrating on the mind. This won't be the traditional psych class. We won't just study terms and the ideas of psychology. We'll get into the practical application. Do you know what kind of person you are? Do you know why you think the way you think?"

As I was listening to him lecture, I knew I didn't understand myself. It was the first day of school, and I felt strange things I had never felt before. My gut was twisting and turning. Not even at my prom, graduation, and debutante ball did I experience that. Maybe Mr. O'Conner was going to help me find out why.

"All right, Cammie, I'll talk to you later," I said as we headed in different directions.

Deep down, I guess I wanted a best friend to replace the ones that were dear to my heart in high school. Though I didn't know Cammie well, I wasn't feeling that she was the one. However, I agreed that we'd hook up later, and who knew, maybe my initial thoughts would be wrong.

I was now headed to English class—literature, to be exact. I was not looking forward to it at all. In high school we did some Shakespeare, but most of the books were Toni Morrison and stuff on that line that were more cultural and relevant to our past as well as our future as African-Americans. So the whole sonnets thing was going to be new to me.

"Excuse me," I heard over my shoulder. I wasn't sure the person was talking to me so I kept looking forward. "Excuse me." I turned around, and it was a redheaded girl sitting beside a brunette. They were both adorably cute.

"Are you talking to me?" I questioned, totally not thinking they were.

"Yeah. We just wanted to tell you your shoes are so cute. They look so comfortable. I'm Chrissy, and this is Megan," the redhead said. "We were just in your psychology class. We were probably looking at your shoes more than we listened to the professor."

I was thinking, *Blake and Shanay talked about these same shoes. Two other people think they are adorable. Wow! Good thing I'm confident in my style and not trying to be swayed by the thoughts of others, or I never would have received this compliment.*

"Thank you," I said to them. "I don't know where my mom got them, but they are very comfortable. I think they are stylish."

"They are," Chrissy said. "You can move back one and sit beside us if you want."

Since the room was still filling up, and I didn't know anyone coming in, I took them up on their offer and really enjoyed the interaction. As we waited for class to begin, we giggled and chatted. I was totally outside of my comfort zone, yet I was totally comfortable with these girls. Don't get me wrong; we weren't down. It wasn't that sort of thing, but it was totally natural. And I liked that.

We weren't really talking about much of anything—clothes, shoes, hairstyles, television shows, and trends. We liked the same things and that was cool. When I think about it, they were cool, and I was glad I didn't let my initial barrier keep me closed into my own social circle. Talking to these strangers assured me that there were rewards for stepping outside of your own boundaries.

I understand why people never do it. Taking that first step is so hard. Who wants to fail or fall and risk being embarrassed and not having their friendship accepted or their hands shaken when they extend it? If you never try to make a new friend, you'll never add one to your list. Chrissy and Megan taught me that lesson, and I will never forget it. It was appropriate that we were in English lit class because, for sure, you can't judge a book by its cover.

So maybe it would be the same with the reading list that I noticed as I checked over the syllabus for the quarter. Maybe some of the stuff would bring me joy and expand my mind. That's what it's all about anyway. Not being the same Payton that came here. Not leaving with only a degree, but also leaving more complete than I came in.

Two days later in English literature class, Chrissy and Megan were waiting on me.

"Hey, Payton," Megan called out.

"Hey, y'all."

It was a warm reception. We had literature on Mondays, Tuesdays, and Thursdays. Psychology was on Mondays and Wednesdays.

Our teacher, Professor Bissett, summoned us to write a one-page essay during the class period. The title was "Expectations as a Freshman at UGA." I didn't even know if I'd complete the assignment, because I started the paper three times before I finally got a clue as to what to say. Searching my soul, I realized I didn't know what I expected. For so long, I had just wanted to be on my own, away from home and in college. I never gave much thought to what I wanted when I got there. Yeah, I knew my ultimate goal. But the process by which that end becomes reality, the stuff in the middle, the stuff that gets you from point A to point B, is the stuff that stumped me. What did I expect as a freshman? Did I have expectations?

My paper read:

In answering the question of what do I expect as a freshman at UGA, I am thrown for a loop. That is because maybe the thing that I am thinking about has nothing to do with why my parents sent me here. As I wrestle within, I have to be truthful and honest and say that I want to fit in. Yet, how can I fit in when even in this very room I see no one like me? I do fit in with these two strangers with whom the world would probably say I'm not a match. However, I'm like a hand in a glove with them. We talk about things that teens talk about.

I want love, and I couldn't find it in high school, or as soon as I had it in my hand it slipped away like a baseball sometimes does in a catcher's hand. But the ball had carried on to Georgia. Thus, I'm chasing that ball, hoping not to miss an opportunity to feel my heart beat for love. I expect to grow. There is pain, stretching of bones, and tugging of large muscles, and I don't know if I have thought about it before now.

I expected things to be easy. I've only been here a week, and I realize that things are not easy at all. My dad once told me that the hardest things in life were most rewarding once you accomplish them. But what am I trying to accomplish as a freshman? Trying to just survive? Yeah, maybe that's it. I just want to survive. I want to be an overcomer. I don't want to go home with my tail tucked between my legs feeling ashamed that I failed or feeling like I didn't want to be here. Yet, I want to break free of this cocoon I'm in, as I learn my way and change from a high school student to a college freshman. I just want to get my wings, be as beautiful as a butterfly, and take off.

I expect that to happen soon. What am I going to do to make it happen? I don't know. Am I willing to do what it takes to reach that goal? Maybe. Am I on the right track? Who knows? This paper may sound confusing, but right now I am feeling so many different things that I am confused. So back to the original question, expectations of a college freshman at UGA, I expect to figure it out along the way.

I got out of my seat and noticed I was the last one in the class. I handed my paper to Professor Bissett. She said, "Well, Payton Skky, you seem to be writing rather intensely. I'm sure it's gonna be a great read."

Humbly I replied, "I sure hope so, Professor. I definitely wrote from the soul."

"Do you mind if I sit here?" I said to a milk-chocolate sistah.

She appeared so sad. Though I wasn't ecstatic, I wasn't sad, at least not on that particular day. She didn't want to talk. I was hungry and didn't want to talk until I had a bite to eat. I probably looked unpolished with my table etiquette as I talked with my mouth full.

I said, "Girl, what's wrong?"

She still didn't respond.

"I understand," I said. "I miss home, too. The first couple of days have been overwhelming, but I've been dealin' with it. So I can understand being tired of all this. I've got so much homework, but I wanna go shopping and go to a party, and I wanna do so much stuff. I'm loaded down with books. So you don't even have to say it. I feel you. I know what you're thinking."

"You don't know a thing about me," she finally blurted out hastily.

I wasn't expecting the words she spoke.

"You're not feeling that stuff? You're not overwhelmed? See, you're doin' good," I told her.

"No, you don't understand. I'm not doin' good. I wish I had your problems, not able to go shopping and not going to parties, because you gotta get a higher education. I don't even have my high school diploma."

Once she said that, I knew I must have not heard her right, because how could she be in college with no high school diploma?

She went on to say she was one of the cafeteria staff. She didn't have on her white lunchroom coat, so how was I supposed to know? I wanted to ask her why she didn't graduate, but I didn't want to get in her business. I always had a way of thinking I could help people, but I always take them to places they don't want to go and see my way into places that they don't want me to see.

So I said, "I'm sorry; I'll just eat and mind my business."

When I turned away, she totally opened up, telling me that a year ago, she was a senior in high school, but in the early part of the year she got pregnant. Not by her boyfriend, but by some guy that she had liked all through high school who finally gave her the time of day. Not just one time, but a couple of times. He played the role to the hilt, and she was the leading lady. One day he got tired of her, but it was too late—she was already pregnant.

Immediately my mind flashed back to the time when my girlfriend Lynzi told me she thought she was pregnant. How frightening! Immediately we knew that if she had the baby she could go on to finish her degree. So many people do, but so many people drop out like this girl sitting right here beside me. If I hadn't said no to Dakari, I might have been where she is. Though it's not the end of the world, it's not a great place to be.

She had serious issues, and my little drama of wanting to go here and there and not being able to because I had obligations of studying were nothing. She had obligations to a baby. At seventeen she wanted to go here and there, and should be able to, but couldn't because she's a mother. It made me realize I was so glad I stayed pure and followed God as opposed to following my flesh and desires. Sure, that guy made her feel good and made her feel important while he was loving on her and telling her things that she wanted to hear. The moment was right; she seized it. After that moment was over, the consequences were so great because she didn't do it God's way. She was still suffering from her poor choice.

"Would you mind if I asked you a question?"

"Sure, go ahead. I told you this much," she said as she gestured for me to talk.

"Why did you drop out of school?"

"Because I was overwhelmed. I didn't have no money to put my baby in day care. It was just me, my mom, and my two little sisters. They had to stay in school, and I couldn't. I had already done one thing wrong with being physically involved with this guy, so I didn't want to make another mistake. No way was I going to have an abortion. My mama had me young. What if she had made that choice to abort? I wouldn't even be here telling you this."

"Wow, you right!" I commented, absolutely amazed at her strength.

She continued, "So I went ahead and had my baby. Don't get me wrong, I love my boo. I got a little boy. Girrrl, he is so cute. But it's a lot, and I am just a kid myself. I remember my aunts trying to tell me that, and they were right. I am too young to be a mom. I'm doing good as a mom. I got a job right now, but this was not the way I wanted my life to go. I wanted it to be better than my mom's. She had me at sixteen, and I had my baby at seventeen, which is still too young. I can't look back at that. Before you walked over here, I was looking at all you college kids, wishing it was me. It was supposed to be me. That's why I looked sad. What's your name?"

"Payton."

"Hi, Payton, I'm Drea. I wish I had your problems. So make the most of this college thang. Don't go down the wrong track. It might be hard. It might be different, but at least you have the opportunity to make it work. Don't blow this chance. I'm working in the cafeteria, but I'm thankful I've got a job. There's nothing wrong with working in a cafeteria. My mom does that, but when you wanna be a doctor . . . "

"You still can be a doctor," I cut in.

"Well, yeah, but it will be harder now."

"And so? What does that mean? You just told me that when it gets hard, keep going. Now I'm telling you. You don't know the stories of all the kids here. Some barely got into Georgia and some are here but wanted to go somewhere else. Some probably got a loan that will take them who knows how long to pay. Some got two ex-boyfriends here and still like both of them."

"Girl, is that you?"

"Yeah, we'll have to talk," I replied as if it was a really long story.

This girl, Drea, reminded me of Dymond. Her family wasn't from the best side of the tracks—just trying to make it from meal to meal. Doing the best they could, but good at heart. As I sat there and talked to Drea, I realized that although I was in college and she wasn't, I was no better than her. God made both of us, and He loves both of us.

As I was feeling overwhelmed with my circumstances, I was so glad I had a God that stayed close to me when I strayed away from Him. He brought this diamond in the rough to show me that it could be worse. I was learning. I was getting better. I was feeling more than I ever had. I had let myself learn from the world around me. Here I was thinking that I knew it all. My hand was open to what God wanted to put in it. He was allowing me to meet new people, and, through Drea, He was allowing me to realize that I was experiencing new emotions.

5

Laboring
for Love

"So, what do I have to do to get a date with you, Payton?"
my bow-tie-wearing friend asked over the phone Friday
evening.

I never gave Karlton my phone number. He just called
information and got it. He called me every day that week
and asked about going to the movies.

"You're silly, Karlton. What do you mean, what do you
have to do to get me to go? It's been a crazy week getting
adjusted to new surroundings. I didn't put you off because
I didn't want to go out with you. I hope you understand
that."

Karlton persisted,"So, if that's the case, and it's the weekend, then why don't you go with me?"

"Well, it's already six-thirty."

"Yeah, and there's a seven o'clock movie. I'm right outside of your dorm room. We can make it if you come now."

I huffed. It was mighty forward of him to just assume
that I'd go. Outside of my dorm room? I didn't know whether

to be flattered or if that was just creepy. But because I was expanding my horizons, I quickly threw on something cute out of the closet, that was already pressed. I passed Laurel's bed without leaving a note and headed out the door.

When I got out to the parking lot, I chuckled on the inside when I saw Karlton for the first time without a tie. He actually looked quite suave. Five-eleven frame, caramel complexion, wavy hair, contacts. The brotha looked different, and the view before me was quite appealing.

As he walked around to his side of the car, I quickly thought, *Darn, I'm going out with a junior! Big time; I got it goin' on!*

When I got into the car and the door locked, I quickly realized that this might not be the safest thing in the world. I didn't know where his dorm was or if he was staying in an apartment. I didn't know his roommates or much about him. Nobody had seen me leave with him, so if something happened there would be no witnesses. Karlton could have just been playing me, acting all nice to get me in his car and then do anything. I thought so little of myself to just be swayed by sweet words. I was responsible for anything that could happen to me, both good and bad.

"You seem so tense," he said as he tried placing his hand behind my neck.

Quickly I drifted out of his grasp. How dare he try to touch me! Now I was on the defensive.

"There you go again, making it hard for me to get close to you. What's all that about? I thought you were such a sweet girl, Payton Skky. You don't want to give me a chance? I'm not going to bite."

"Give you a chance with what? I'm in your car with you going to the movies. You don't have to touch me. We don't have to hold hands on this date."

He moved his arm back over to the steering wheel. Now I was really uncomfortable. I had gotten him on edge. This wasn't a good idea. Though deep, deep, deep down inside I didn't really think anything serious would happen to me, that was just a guess. I didn't really know. Fortunately, the movie theater wasn't too far from campus.

When we got out, I said, "You can get the tickets. I'll meet you at the door. I'm just going to fix my face."

Though I cared about how I looked, that wasn't an issue. I grabbed my cell phone out of my purse, went behind his car, and dialed Laurel's number in our room. I left her a message:

"Laurel. Hey, it's Payton. I'm out on a date with that guy we met from SGA last week. He had on the bow tie and the glasses. Well, he doesn't have on any of that tonight, and his license plate number is K53-668. We're at the movies, and I should be home right after. If I don't come home, call the police. I think he's cool, but I'm not sure. I just wanted to touch base to let you know where I am. So I hope you are having fun with your sorority sisters. All right, bye," I quickly uttered into the receiver.

On my way from the parking lot I noticed a very familiar car. It was Tad's, parked just as neat and straight as always. I wondered why he was there.

Oh, my gosh! I can't let him see me out on a date. Ohhh, I thought. But what is he doing here? It's Friday night. Doesn't he have a game that's out of town?

Then I realized that I had not been in touch with Tad or Dakari all week. I never knew their football schedule, and I didn't want to call them too late. Plus, I wanted to get back to the mentality of girls not calling guys. I just figured if they wanted to talk, they knew my number, and they could call me. I didn't want to let them know that they were heavily on my mind.

"There you are," Karlton said as he placed his arm around my waist.

There it was again. That uncomfortable feeling. I hardly

knew this guy, and though he looked cute and was an upperclassman, I wasn't trying to go there. I didn't want to send the wrong signals.

Slyly moving away from him I said, "So, what movie are we going to see?"

"A romance flick. I thought you'd like that."

"Actually, I like action."

"Well, too late. I already bought the tickets. What about popcorn?"

"Yeah, popcorn is good. Why don't I wait for you inside the theater? It's getting kind of crowded. Everybody's out to see a show on Friday night."

I sat down toward the back, rationalizing that, though the lights were on, Karlton might not be able to find me. I wanted to make it as easy as possible and be on the lookout for him when he walked in. When I turned around so that he could see me, I was stunned when I laid eyes on Tad and a little short, long-haired, red bone.

Who's she? I thought.

They walked right past me. They seemed to be having a good time laughing and joking. I felt like a spy as I watched them go to their seats. They kept laughing, and it grew louder and very irritating. I had no clue what could be so funny, but Tad seemed entertained by her.

They sat four rows up, and since no one was in front of me I got a clear view of their interaction. There was some type of chemistry, but what was the spark about? I knew he wasn't over me. He had just told me last week. Though he was going through it, and I wasn't really there for him, I had my own drama. So as soon as I didn't give Tad 100 percent, he went to find somebody else?

Oh, cut it out, Payton. You don't even know what's going on, I told myself as I tried desperately to hold on.

Before I could totally get upset, Karlton sat down. "Popcorn, my lady?"

All during the movie, I wondered if I should get up, go sit beside Tad, and strike some fear in his heart. Maybe I should let him see me with Karlton at the end. I could quickly get out of there and not let him know I was there. I had no idea of what to do or where to go, and before I could really think about it, the situation just happened. The movie was over, and I tried to get up immediately and leave, but Karlton, who was on the side closest to the exit, took his time reading the credits.

Karlton did tell me in the car that he was thinking about going to film school after he finished Georgia. So I understood why he was studying the craft. However, I had to get out of there. I didn't want my ex-boyfriend to see me, but as soon as we stood up to walk out, Tad and his date passed our row.

"Hi," I said as his face met mine.

Somehow I had gotten separated from Karlton, and it appeared as if I was alone.

"Hey," Tad said, a little taken back that I was there. "What are you doing out this time of night alone?"

Oh, he had to go there and call me out because he was on a date. Like I couldn't get one or something. I quickly let the brotha know that I was not alone. He wasn't the only one who could attract someone else.

"Can you let me by so I can get to my date? He's waiting at the door. Thank you," I said as I brushed by him rudely.

On the way home, Karlton asked me repeatedly if I wanted to go and get something to eat. I didn't understand why he couldn't accept that I didn't want anything. All I wanted to do was go home to my dorm room and cry into my pillow. Though I didn't say how down I was, I was persistent in saying no, so I didn't understand why we ended up at Checkers.

"Can you take me home now?" I asked him after he gobbled down two chili dogs.

"Why are you in such a rush? Why are you not letting me get to know you? Why are you making me work so hard? I've thought about you since I met you. You're different than a lot of other freshmen that I come into contact with."

"Is that what appealed to you? That I had my mind in other places? Do you think girls just look at your face and think you're so cute and do whatever you want them to do? So that doesn't attract you when someone has their own mind and wants to do their own thing. You're attracted because they give you little resistance?"

"Where is this coming from, Payton?" he asked.

I didn't know where it was coming from, so I couldn't answer him. I was just going through it, and I didn't know why. I thought I just wanted to be friends with Tad. Dakari gets a girl, I wanna be with him. Tad gets a girl, I wanna be with him. You never know, maybe if I saw Karlton with somebody else next week I would wanna be with him.

Oh, Lord, help me, I prayed. *I don't know what I want or who I want. And I am quite angry right now. I might have blown it. Tad's the only guy who ever cared about me. Even as I listen to Karlton's reasons to want to be with me, they have nothing to do with You, but everything to do with me. I blew it.*

Thanks, Lord, I thought as I got home and snuggled between the sheets. *Thanks for letting my instinct be right this time. I'm definitely going to be more careful next time. Though Karlton was a gentleman, I don't think he is my type. If he is, don't let me blow it.*

I woke up early the next morning with images of the girl that Tad was with planted firmly in my mind. I had to admit, she was cute. The more I concentrated on the image of this girl, the more I realized there was something unique about her. Something extraspecial. She had a diamond cross around her neck. That thing was sparkling, but it was a cross. She was probably a Christian, and that's probably what appealed to Tad. Duh! She was walking the walk, unlike me.

I knew Dakari wouldn't be in the room to answer the phone since the team was out of town. Since Tad was out last night, surely he didn't travel with the team. So I went against my beliefs and dialed his number.

"Yeah," he said.

"Get up, sleepyhead."

"Oh, so now you're gonna talk to me?"

"I apologize. I was a little harsh, but I didn't know I was going to see you out."

"What's the big deal, Payton? You were out."

"Yeah, but you thought I was alone."

"But you weren't alone, were you, Payton?"

"What difference does it make? You weren't alone, either."

"Payton, you called me. Was there some point to this call? I don't wanna go back and forth with who was out and who wasn't. Now . . . we're bigger than that. It's not like it matters anymore. We're just friends, right, Payton? Hello?"

"Well, I don't know if I just want to be friends," I mumbled, almost crying.

"Payton, you don't know if you want to be more than friends, either. When you figure it out, then maybe we can talk, but for now, I'm moving on with my life. It ain't about hurting you. It's not about who you were with at the movies. I wanted to see an action flick anyway. Vonda was the one who wanted to see that."

"Vonda? Oh, Vonda is her name?"

Quickly I remembered I didn't want to see that movie either. Tad and I should have just gone out on the date, and we would have been seeing the action picture.

"Payton, come on. Don't be childish. Her name is Vonda. She's really nice and sweet, and she's a Christian. She's a sophomore. She's from South Carolina, too. That's why we hooked up."

"She's from your hometown?"

"She didn't go to Silver Bluff, but all the surrounding towns are so small, I know her."

Well, that's just great, I thought. *They have history.* Besides, she was a Christian.

"What does she have that I don't? Why are you so attracted to her?"

"What are you talking about? We were just out on a date."

"Yeah, but y'all were laughing and everything. I saw it."

"What do you mean, you saw it? Saw what?"

"I was sitting behind you, and I noticed you when you first sat down together. Y'all were really laughing. You seem to be diggin' her, this Honda person! Do you like her because she is prettier than me? Because her hair is longer? Because of her body?"

"Don't even go there, Payton. This isn't about any of that stuff. But I guess right now I can say that she's not as pretty as you. Though we're good friends, she's been praying with me because things have been a little rough. I'm not traveling with the team, if you haven't noticed. Our second game is today, and the team is away, and I'm at home. I'm in the bed instead of hearing the talk from the coach. I'm not getting ready. I'm not preparing for a game. I'm sitting in this empty dorm room. I'm one of only six players here. I didn't know I needed somebody to talk to. However, we kind of bumped into each other. We've just been praying. It's just about that, not about her and me. Just about that."

There was dead silence. I didn't know what to say. Tad kept talking.

"Last night we wanted to go to the movies to get our

minds off things. Her dad died last month, in the same week as her grandmother," he said. "So she's really dealing with it, and she can understand my struggles with my grandmother, too. We bonded. Not that I feel I owe you an explanation, but since you gotta know all my business."

"Well, I'm sorry I'm bothering you. Go back to sleep. 'Bye."

I hung up. As I lay back in my bed, I realized that I was tripping. Tripping really hard.

Oh, Lord, I am trippin'. Hanging up on him. Spying on him, wanting him. Help me, Lord. Help me. I'm trippin'.

Why am I here? I thought as I looked around and saw mostly white people.

Laurel had talked me into going with her to one of the fraternity houses to watch the football game on the big screen. I was really being ignored. Not that I cared. I didn't fit in there, and I didn't want to fit in. She needed me to come because her ex-boyfriend, Branson, belonged to that particular fraternity. If anyone understood how tough it was to get over exes, it was me. So, I went there to help her out.

"Go! Go! Go!" I yelled as I forgot my surroundings when I saw Dakari run from one end of the field to the other on a kickoff return.

This was the second game and his second special-teams, touchdown.

"Go! That's my boy!" I said.

Everyone looked at me for a moment like I had lost my mind. Or maybe I was simply being paranoid. I didn't care.

Then, one of the fraternity guys who I think was the president said, "Do you know him?"

Laurel cut in and said, "Yeah, they went to the same high school together. They're really tight."

72

One person asked, "Are you Dakari Graham's girl-friend?"

Before I could respond, someone else said, "Oh, my gosh! She's here."

I was the most popular person sitting in that fraternity house, the little black girl. Just because I knew a football player who scored a touchdown, everybody wanted to talk to me. Crazy, but true. Before I could even say Dakari wasn't my boyfriend, I got asked tons of questions. I had just realized at that moment what a big deal Georgia football is.

"Can I get you something to drink? A beer?" someone asked.

"No, thank you. Coke is it for me. I don't drink."

"Oh, sorry, I'll be right back with a Coca-Cola." The guy then walked to the back.

Laurel quickly came up to me and said, "That's Branson. He's getting you a Coke. Talk to him for me, please. Payton, talk to him."

"That was Branson? Ohhh . . . I can't talk to him for you," I looked at her and said.

"Yes, you can. These people like you now. Talk to him, please!"

When he came back, I said, "Hey! Sit down. Watch the game with me."

"Sure," he said as he sat down next to me.

I couldn't believe how willing I was to go to battle for my roommate. The way this guy dogged her out, why in the world would she want him back? But as I thought about it, I realized that the same ballplayer that had just run up and down the field only a year ago had broken my heart in a similar way. A part of me wanted him back. Why? So stupid, but real.

It was more clear to me then: Just as I knew Laurel did not need to be back with Branson, I also realized I did not need to be back with Dakari. Sure, he was doing good in ball, but who cared? Though it seemed like the whole university did at that moment, I didn't need to be a part of that massive crowd. I needed to be friends with Dakari, and that's what Laurel needed to be with Branson. If anybody understood that a person has got to learn the hard way, it was me. So I did what I said I would do and tried to get them back together.

"You know, I came here with Laurel Shadrach. The name ring a bell?" I probed as the look on Branson's face remained unchanged. "Why are you making this difficult? You know she still likes you."

He shrugged. As I saw where he was looking, I noticed two girls leaning up against the bar. They were smiling and talking about him. I could tell he had it going on in this circle.

"OK, quit looking at the girls. I'm talking to you."

When I had his undivided attention, I wanted to plead Laurel's case. Branson spoke instead. "Correct me if I'm wrong, but I think the term is, 'Been there and been with that.' I'm in college, and I'm moving on. If you care about Laurel, help her to get over me, because I don't want her anymore. If you want to talk about football, we can talk now. If you want to talk about school, catch me on Monday. But if you want to talk about her, I'm not the one you need to be talking to. I don't mean any disrespect or anything. You seem pretty nice, but I'm through with that. But if you need another drink, you just let me know."

I saw Laurel rushing over to me. "What did he say?"

"We'll talk about it later."

I didn't know how to break it to her. I didn't know how to break her heart. I didn't know how to tell her that she had to move on. That she'd be able to survive when I couldn't. So I said nothing and just played it off and watched the rest of the game.

"You guys can come and eat. Your dad is finished with the ribs," my mom said to Rain and me as we lay across my bed at home. Oh, what a comfortable bed it was.

It was Labor Day, and my parents were having a big barbecue. I had come home, and Rain happened to be home, too, so I invited her over. Most of the day she had talked about how fun Spelman was. I was happy for her. I truly was. I was going through it, my roommate was going through it, and Tad was going through it. I had issues, and I just needed to talk.

"So I don't know if Tad still likes me," I said after I told her all of it.

"You shouldn't have hung up on him."

"I know I shouldn't have hung up on him, but I did. I haven't talked to him since."

"Well, you came here, and you've been here since Saturday night. It's Monday. You never know; he may have called."

"I checked my machine. Rain, he hasn't called. Don't think it," I said, cutting her off. "I'm not calling again. Every time I break the rule about calling guys, bad stuff happens. Now I see why my dad told me not to call those jerks."

"So now Tad's a jerk?" Rain teased.

I tossed a pillow at her head, and she threw one back at me.

"Barbecue's getting cold," my mom said.

"We're coming!" I yelled back.

It felt so good to be back home. It felt like high school again. It wasn't high school days anymore. In a few hours, I'd be driving back to my new world. A world that was spinning desperately around me, and I wanted it to stop.

"Well, I'm going downstairs to get some of your dad's good barbecue."

"I'll be down in a second."

Before I could look up, my mom had entered my room and sat down on my bed. She seemed serious. I hoped things were OK.

She asked me what was wrong. "You've been in school a while, and you haven't called. Is everything OK?"

I didn't know how to let my mom inside, and I didn't want her to worry, so I tried to act hard on the outside.

"I could use a hug," I said to her.

Without question, she wrapped her arms around me extremely tight. Tears flowed down my face, resembling a waterfall. I was so unsure, so insecure, so unstable. But in her embrace there was an ounce of relief.

"I love you, Mommy. I just wanna make you proud of me."

"I am proud of you. The fact that you've gone to school, that you're doing good work, that you're responsible—I am proud of you, Payton. Just keep God in the forefront of your mind. I know it might seem overwhelming, and the level of academics has stepped up a notch, but if you apply yourself, you can do it. I realize that both Mr. Graham and Mr. Taylor are now at your school."

My mom had never mentioned the two of them before.

"Yeah, don't be surprised," she said, being down. "I'm a woman. Cute young boys who have their heads on sort of straight—I can understand the attraction that you might feel. I'm challenging you. You are still way too young to be thinking about anything serious. You're in a new place. You need to get adjusted to that. You don't need to get into the dynamics of a relationship."

"Mom!" I said, getting frustrated when I should have been listening.

"OK, you be hardheaded and think you know it all and get yourself in trouble up there. I'm trying to tell you. Those boys are thinking about their scholarships, and you need to be thinking about making sure you stay in school, as well.

It's tough enough to work for good grades; you don't need to work for anything else right now. I know we don't talk about this tough stuff, but I'm here for you. I'm just a phone call away. You have the calling-card number. You know how to use it when you want money. Use it when you need your mom."

She kissed me on the forehead and walked out of the door. Oh, how I didn't want to go back to school. The first week, though not miserable, was surely not what I had in mind all those years when I wanted to be anywhere but at home.

When I got back, I had to have a tough conversation with Laurel. I would have given anything to have not been the bearer of bad tidings.

Karlton, whom I hadn't thanked for our date, had called several times when I checked the messages. I just didn't know what I wanted to say to him. My mom was right about the schoolwork. It was somewhat overwhelming. I had to find a new way of studying because my old way of just reading the material and doing the homework wasn't going to cut it on this level. I was going to have to study every subject every night.

Then there was Tad, a guy after God's own heart. He was dealing with some of his own disappointment, going from superstar in high school to not even being able to ride the bench in college. He needed Christian love and support. I didn't know if I could give it to him. How could I give him something I didn't have? My relationship with the Lord seemed stale and cold. Yet in my heart, I so wanted that to change.

One thing was for sure, Laurel and I were in the same place. We were miserable when it came to guys. Maybe that common bond was going to get her through what I was about to say. We were both too young to be stressed. We were freshmen in college with four bright years ahead of us. Yeah, that's what I was going to tell her. We were too young to be laboring for love.

6

Trying Out Churches

"There you are, Payton," Laurel said as she grabbed some of the bags out of my arms and helped me to the chair.

She sat down next to me on her bed, opened the refrigerator, and popped a Coke for me. She wanted to hear about Branson badly. I guess she thought the news that I was going to give her would make her night, but I knew full well it would definitely be the opposite of that. I had just gotten back from Augusta. Surely this could have waited.

Lord, give me the words to say to this girl. I'm about to break her heart. This is not going to be easy. Help me make it medicine to her soul. Please, Lord, I prayed as I took a sip from the cold, refreshing drink.

"Why are you hesitating? It's not good news, is it? He doesn't want to be with me, huh? Well, did you tell him how much I still loved him? How much I still cared?" With her head hanging low, she continued, "Sometimes I'm tempted to say I'd be willing. . ."

"Listen to yourself," I said to her as I put down the

Coke. "Don't belittle your beliefs to keep Branson. He's a jerk, and you're worth way more than he could offer or give."

"It's easy for you to say, Payton. You're moving on with your life. I just got a message from you the other day saying you were out on a date. I can't go out on dates. It's not that easy for me to meet somebody new."

"You've had somebody new before. Why can't you do it again?"

Laurel told me that she liked someone from her high school. However, it was clear that she didn't want to talk about it. So I tried to encourage and not push.

"Why do you think that? Look at you." I stood, pulled her from the bed and over to the mirror we had on the back of our closet door. "I see a beautiful girl with gorgeous hair, a wonderful personality; and any guy, including Branson, would be stupid to pass you up. If he does, it will be his loss. Move on. As my friends say, 'You got it goin' on. Later for that brotha.' Well, maybe he's not a brotha, but you know what I'm sayin'."

I was trying to be silly. Secretly, I was hoping she would grab hold of my comical attitude and push past the pain. Unfortunately, that wasn't the case.

She fell to the floor and let out uncontrollable sobs. I had no idea college was going to be this hard. And though I didn't want to be dealt this hand, as I looked down at my new friend in her dark hour, I knew I had to step in. I had to find some way to pull her out of this. On my way home to the dorm, I'd noticed a church was having a revival. If we got dressed, we could make it. Maybe that's what we both needed, a revival—and renewal. We needed to look to God and trust Him instead of ourselves to find this hope. Get rid of some of that junk and cling to some hope. Hope that only a heavenly Father could bring.

I don't know how I convinced Laurel to go. We sat in a

small church that was packed. I could tell Laurel was uncomfortable. She was the only white person there. It was a small, black country church. As soon as people started jumping around and dancing in the aisles and screaming "Hallelujah," without the preacher saying anything, I started to get a little uncomfortable myself.

Now, don't get me wrong. I wasn't an uppity black Christian or anything, but this just wasn't my style. People laying hands on folks, pushing them to the floor. I had seen it on TV but never up close before. I wondered if there really was true inner healing going on, or if it was just a show.

As the music grew louder and louder, Laurel started to look around. She clutched her purse tightly. *What was that about?* I wondered.

"They ain't gonna take nothin'," I said to her, quite irritated.

Quietly Laurel asked, "Is your church at home like this?"

I noticed two women being fanned by ushers because they had the Spirit, and I said, "No, my church at home isn't like this."

But before I could get all worked up and feel that this was beneath me and that I could never find God in this little cubbyhole, something came over me. I wouldn't have been led here unless God wanted to teach me something. So as the pastor got up to preach, I listened intently.

"Church," the tall, dark-skinned man with the royal blue robe said, "I want to talk about Philippians. Church, if you would turn your Bible to the fourth chapter."

He was talking about Philippians 4:13: "I can do all things through Christ who strengthens me."

As I realized that both Laurel and I had some real problems with our self-image, I knew why we were sent here. Both of us had gotten so wrapped up in ourselves—our body, our skills, our talents, and our attractiveness to others—that we forgot to focus on God. This little country pastor was going to speak to us. We both needed to hear his words.

"I can do all things through Christ who strengthens me. I can, I can, I can do all things through Christ who strengthens me. I can do all things through my Christ who gives me strength," the pastor echoed. "As we have another school year upon us, I found myself asking the Lord, 'Lord, what do You want me to tell the church? What do You want me to tell my children as they prepare to go back to school? How can I prepare the members of Bald Rock Baptist Church to be more than conquerors in You?' And Church, He led me to this passage, and this passage is hope for us all!"

"Amen!" someone shouted from the back of the room.

There was no air conditioning, and fans were going back and forth across the room. Earlier, I was sweating, but at that moment sweat was not a thought. *Hope for us all*. His last words were lingering in my head. *Talk, Pastor; I want to hear what you have to say. Preach on.*

"When our kids go back to school, you go back to your job, and the newness of everything sets in, situations may be somewhat difficult. I encourage you to keep your eyes on Jesus Christ. To know when it's hard to get out of the bed because all summer long you have been sleeping until the noonday hour. When your alarm clock goes off, and you have no strength, and you want to stay under the covers, you need to make sure you pray. Pray something like, 'Lord, thanks for waking me up this morning and for starting me on my way.' Somehow, someway, the Lord will blow wind into your body and raise you up. The mere thought that you started with Him in mind means that it is going to be a great day with endless possibilities."

He was coming to the end of his sermon, and out of the corner of my eye, I saw Laurel smile at me the same way I smiled at her. I couldn't see us worshiping at this church on a regular basis, but on that night, a night when we had no words to encourage each other, the Lord led us to Bald Rock. As the pastor closed out his service, I was so glad that He led us there, because I was truly being fed.

"So, Church, when you feel things don't go the way you want them to, when you feel you don't know how stuff will work out, when you feel you are down and depressed because your future looks anything but bright, believe in the One who is within you. Know that the Holy Spirit will work it out. Know that He will give you what you need, and He will show you the plan. Be encouraged, saints. If you're with Him, He will give you hope. So hold on. It says in Matthew with man this is impossible, but with God all things are possible."

On our way out of the building, Laurel and I were hand in hand. We stopped to let the pastor know how much he had blessed us. As we left Bald Rock, we both had hope.

Two days later, I was sitting with Dakari in the guest area of my dorm. He had called and said he needed to see me right away. We hadn't talked since his game on Saturday when he had scored another exploding touchdown. The boy was bad. He had a couple of interviews in the local paper. He was on Coach Eckerds's television show, and a lot of people on campus were starting to recognize him. I could tell that firsthand as girls walked by and squealed at his presence.

"So, you're just a big-time celebrity now, huh?" I teased him.

"Yeah, yeah, they give me some recognition. You know, Payton, I never thought that I would get to play on this level this early. My brother didn't even line up until his sophomore year. My parents are proud."

I questioned, "What about you? Are you proud of yourself?"

"No doubt, no doubt," he said with confidence, "but what I wanted to talk to you about is your boy."

I huffed because I knew he was going to mention Tad. Tad and I hadn't talked since I saw him at the movies that Friday night. I might have been one of the last people that could give advice about what was going on with Tad, but I listened anyway.

"He's been moping around the room. He's been playa hatin' basically."

"What do you mean?" I asked.

"Well, you know, because I'm getting to play. Though I'm not on offense like I wanna be. I'm in my regular position on special teams, and I'm making some big-time plays that are changing the game around for us. With the field position I give them, I'm in there. To be honest, I thought he would be starting before me. He's got talent in the backfield, but I've really found my niche. After getting over the initial shock of being the deep man, I'm making guys miss."

"Well, I know you, too, Dakari. And you can be very . . . well, how do I say this . . . ?"

"Say it. Just say it. It's just me and you."

"You kind of brag and show off. It's probably got him a little upset."

"Oh, so you're saying that I'm bringing this on myself. C'mon, Payton. I can't go for that. Just talk to him for me. Tell him that his day is coming, and he don't need to front me like that. Besides if he keeps on tryin' to downplay my skills and keeps gettin' all up in my face, then it's gonna be on in our room. He's ain't actin' like no Christian."

"What does his desire to want to play have to do with him being a Christian?"

"I don't know. I guess it's the way he's been handling it. You're suppose to be happy for your brotha, your roommate, your teammate, and if anybody should be actin' jeal-

84

ous, it should have been me. Shoot, I have problems with my own brother," Dakari expressed, "but I'm not there yet. That's out on the table. I'm not saying I believe in God and I love everybody. Yet when people have good stuff going on for them, I don't trip out like he's doing. That's not me. I say what I do. Your boy ain't doin' that. He's being hypercritical. You really need to talk to him. That's why I came over here, and he's really getting on a side that I can't control. Shoot, we can't go at it for real, or we'll get kicked out of school. We don't get any more chances, no matter how good I'm playing. You know that's why we're rooming together now."

Dakari was right. As far as the coach was concerned, the two of them had to coexist or they wouldn't exist on the field. But I wasn't supposed to help in that. It had nothing to do with me.

"And don't you go thinking you have to stay out of this," Dakari said as if he read my mind.

"It doesn't have anything to do with me. This is about football."

"Yeah, but why do you think we have tension in the first place? Because of you and old high school stuff. I'm past it, and I've moved on, but he still likes you. I can respect that because you're a great woman."

I wanted to say, "Oh, and you don't like me?" but before I could, my suite mate Jewels walked up, throwing her red hair from one side to the other.

"Payton! This is your boyfriend. We saw you the other day. When Payton came up to the fraternity house to watch the game on TV, and you scored, she just told everybody how in love the two of you are."

I looked at her as if she were clearly out of her mind. I wanted to snatch her up out of Dakari's face. She was clearly exaggerating the truth.

"Girlfriend? We're good friends, but I'm free," Dakari said, trying to rap to her.

I couldn't say Jewels was prejudiced, but I remembered when Tad and Dakari broke the window in our dorm room, she thought they were animals. She didn't even want to room with me because she thought that being with me was going to ruin her chances of getting into the sorority of her choice. But I'm not stupid. Dakari is popular, so white or black, if she gets with him, her popularity rises as well. He was such a player. All he cared about was getting as many digits as he could.

Starr Love, you ruined this guy. I thought about the high school chick who came between us. *He was never this ruthless.*

After Starr was finished with Dakari, she went on to date many other guys. Though he never admitted it, I could tell he was really hurt. That's why he tried to get back with me, so he could have someone with substance and quality. He wanted a relationship that meant something, but I guess because I was so wishy-washy he was through with me too. Now that he was balling, he was able to get with a lot of girls, and Jewels was trying to be one of them.

"Payton, you told this girl I was your boyfriend?"

"No, I didn't . . . Why do I have to explain myself? Jewels, we're talking."

Jewels attacked. "So you lied, Payton?"

I was so angry at that moment.

"Well, your stock went down with me, young lady," Jewels said as if her approval made or broke my day.

"I don't have to lie," I told her. "It just got blown out of proportion. I was trying to say ex-boyfriend, and before I knew it people were saying boyfriend. Everybody was just excited about the game."

"Yeah, but you never went back to say that he wasn't your boyfriend. You could have done it when things died down."

"I could have, but I was doing other stuff. Not that I

have to report to you!" I told her. "Dakari, are we finished here?"

I was a little ticked off at him too. How dare he front me in front of her? He didn't know how much of a pain this girl was. Just because he wanted to be with somebody different didn't mean he had to trip with me.

"Well, I'll let you guys talk." Jewels reached into her black Coach backpack and pulled out a black felt-tip pen. She opened up Dakari's hand, and, as if in middle school, she wrote her number in his palm. I wanted to spit in it and erase it, but I did nothing.

She brushed past me. I was about sick of her stunts. She was trying the wrong gal.

"Don't take too long to call me, Dakari. I'm sure that it will be one of the best phone calls you've ever made," she said as she strutted along.

"Oh, so you're into red hair and blue eyes now?" I asked him as I had to practically pick up his tongue and place it back into his mouth.

"No, but you know there wasn't anything like that at Lucy Laney. Now white girls want me. It's a different world, so I might as well explore it."

"Since you're so big and bad and want to explore the world, you need to handle your business and leave me out of it. I've got homework." I got up and walked toward my room.

"Oh, why you gotta be like that?"

"Whatever, Dakari."

Where does time go? I thought as I sat in church that Sunday with Laurel. She had twisted my arm into going to church with her. She said it was only fair since she went with me. Her father had given us a referral. Supposedly, it was like her church at home. It was all stiff and rigid, and all White. I had an attitude for about the first twenty minutes because it wasn't my cup of tea.

As I thought about this not being my style, I remembered my mom told me that one of the past head officers of her sorority once said in a speech that, "Black women are like a tea bag. You never know how strong they are until you put them in a cup of hot water." I equated that to my current situation. My hot water was being stared down by the whole congregation. Everyone was staring except my roommate, who I no longer assumed was naive but know is naive as to prejudices of the world. I started to realize that I had to sit up, be strong, and figure out why God had sent me there. Just like last week when we had gone to Bald Rock Baptist Church, God definitely had some info that I needed to receive.

The members of this church sang the hymns differently than we sang ours. However, I loved singing that day. The meaning was the same no matter which rhythm was used. When they sang "There's a Sweet, Sweet Spirit," I realized that, though different, it was so beautiful, and God was there. When I left the church, He was with me, too, and if He's with me I don't have to be depressed, miserable, or angry or any of the things that are not of the Spirit. I can have true love for all people. Maybe I could tell Tad the same thing.

"Excuse me, why do you always come in here while I'm in the bathroom!"

"Well, you don't lock the door!" I said to Jewels in response to her rudeness.

"Well, actually, Payton, since you are in here, you could tell me what it is that your ex likes and dislikes. Since I am going on a date with him, I wanna make a good impression."

"Well, I guess you better stay here, because if you're gonna go out, the only impression he's gonna get is that you're a . . . I better not even say it because it rhymes with a word I don't wanna use."

"Payton, don't be jealous. It is obvious that you are still infatuated with the guy. I have something that you don't. He's interested in going out with me."

"Believe me, Jewels, if I wanted Dakari I could have him. You are getting my leftovers, and don't you forget that. Now get out of the bathroom; I need to use it. You have a mirror in your room."

"Are you gonna make me?"

"No, but if I have to use it with you in here I'll do that."

"You're so disgusting, Payton," she said as she walked out.

I wouldn't have done that. I knew God wouldn't be pleased with me cutting her down. Oh, that chick was getting on my nerves. I was ticked off that she was going out with Dakari. I would've chosen Shanay over Jewels. This was getting worse and worse, I realized. I had to stay out of Dakari's life. He could do whatever he wanted. If he wanted to be stupid, then that was on him. He was definitely somebody that I didn't need to be with. At least Tad went out on a date with some girl he knew from home. Dakari was getting these fruitcakes off the street.

I was in the bathroom for no more than two minutes. After washing my hands I came out to find Laurel crying once again. This was getting old, really, really old. She was more unhappy than I was, and I was getting sick of it. I didn't want to say anything to her. I just wanted to wave my hand in the air and make it better. But since I had no such magic powers and didn't believe in anything of that kind, I said aloud, "Lord, you need to deal with this because this girl is freaked out."

I grabbed my keys and walked out of the door. I couldn't

handle this. I couldn't deal with this. I could not sit here and listen about this Branson guy one more time. I had had enough.

When I got to the hallway, there was a girl walking around the dorm who seemed lost.

When she got to my door she said, "Excuse me, cleaning lady, I'm looking for . . . "

I stopped her dead in her tracks. "Excuse me? What did you say? I'm a student here."

"Oh, I'm sorry. I thought you were the . . . never mind. Do you live on the first floor? You must be that girl that is suite mate with my sister, Jewels."

Sister, Jewels? Oh, my gosh. Those words almost made me pass out.

"I'm Julie Anne. I'm Jewels's big sister. I'm a junior here. I'm looking for my sister's room."

Though I wanted to go off on this Julie Anne person thinking I was the maid, I just pointed to Jewels's room. Before I could shut my door, she noticed Laurel crying. Julie Anne was an Alpha Gam, too, so she quickly went into my room uninvited and started to comfort Laurel.

"Could you please tell my sister I'm here?" she said to me.

"Yeah, all right," I said.

"I'm trying to get ready," Jewels said sarcastically after hearing the knock.

"Open up," I told her.

"Why'd you come around this way?" Jewels asked. "Why didn't you just come through the bathroom?"

"I was on my way out, and I just came to tell you that your sister is in there with Laurel. She wants you."

"Oh, my gosh, my sister came to visit. I'm going out with Dakari. She will not like that. Please tell her I'm already gone."

"I'm not lying for you. You handle that. 'Bye," I articulated as I turned and walked out of the door.

Jewels wanted to go out with Dakari so that certain people could see her with the big football star, but she didn't want her sister to see her with Dakari the black guy. I was so ticked. And that's what Dakari deserved. He got himself in that mess.

"Hey!" Dakari said to me as I walked past his car. "You sure look nice. Where are you going?"

"Not with you."

"Well, not today, but why don't we go out tomorrow?"

"Dakari, you have got to be out of your mind. You have got to be stupid. I don't know if those other ballplayers have changed you or if you just did this to yourself, but you're crazy. Jewels is in there right now not wanting her sister to see you with her because you're black. You want to go out with her because she's white. This makes no sense," I said, intensely frustrated.

"I don't wanna go out with her just because she's white. I wanna go out with her because she's cute. I ain't gonna take her home to my momma. You know my momma would freak out if I brought home a white girl. So that works both ways. We're just playin' right now, baby. Ain't nothin' serious goin' on. We're havin' a good time. I'll have a good time with you tomorrow if you want."

"Boy, don't make me lose my mind," I said to him.

"Really? It's like that?" he teased back.

"Whatever."

"You see my game yesterday?" he asked.

"Yeah, no touchdown."

"No touchdown, but I had three runbacks, all with seventy yards or more. I might not have scored, but I still had a great game. Oh, but you don't know that much about football, do you?" he said, trying to get smart with me.

"Don't go there with me. I'm not here to get a football degree. I'm here to get an education," I came back at him.

"Dakari, we were on the friends track, but now you are really starting to get on my nerves. You deserve to go out with Jewels. You two are probably gonna have a great time."

As I walked away, I realized that I was becoming good at going off on people. I was an expert at being smart and snappy. That just was not me.

I always wear stuff on my sleeve. I needed to step back and not take things so seriously. What did I care if Dakari dated a white girl? I should be more concerned with a person's salvation than her color. Supposedly, I'd just gotten over that hurdle.

The next week I was really in the same position. Dakari and Jewels were still together. Laurel was still a basket case. Tad still did not have playing time, and I still wasn't digging any of my classes. The situations hadn't changed, and neither had my attitude. I had become more resentful, more bitter, and more angry at everything and everybody. Somebody used my toothpaste, and I went off on all three of my suite mates. They thought the black chick was crazy before—well, now they knew it for certain after I told them not to use my stuff anymore.

I needed counseling. I needed a church home.

Lord, I prayed, *I haven't prayed all week, and it hasn't been a fun one. Probably because I haven't allowed You in it. Today is Sunday, so lead me somewhere to worship.*

After I had gotten out of the shower, I turned on the TV and saw an old pastor my parents love, E. V. Hill, on Trinity Broadcasting Network. He kept saying, "Payday someday, payday someday." I knew I had missed part of the sermon and didn't know what he was talking about, but I just thought if I got connected with Christ, things would work out and that in the end it would all be worth it. However, if

I was in heaven right now and had to testify, the Lord wouldn't be happy about the last couple of weeks of my life. I was so far from Him. My phone rang and interrupted my thoughts.

"Hello," I said, shaken.

"Payton, hey. It's me, Tad."

"Hey," I voiced to him. "What's going on?"

"Well, we've just finished watching film, and I'm trying to catch an eleven o'clock church service. Last week I went to a place called Double Springs Baptist Church, and it was great. I didn't know if you were already gone or if you had church plans, but I'm headed out in about thirty minutes. Do you wanna roll with me?"

"I'd love to," I said.

Hearing his voice was so refreshing, but hearing that he had found a good church home was just what I'd been praying for. I was surprised he wanted me to go with him.

So I asked him in the car, "Why'd you call me? I thought you were mad at me."

"I don't know. We've just been through a lot," he said as he drove us to the church.

He was looking good in his three-piece suit. He was a gorgeous brotha. Although he was troubled within, he was fine without. But on this particular day on the way to church, I wasn't trying to think about all that. So I quickly stopped looking at him and started focusing on why he had called me.

Tad then said, "It just came to me to ask if you wanted to go to church. I don't even know what's been going on with you. I just listened to that voice in my spirit and called you up. You might've hung up on me, but a brotha took a chance."

We laughed. "You are so silly, Tad. I'm sorry for that."

"It's cool."

When we drove into the parking lot of Double Springs

93

Baptist Church, I felt a sense of home. It reminded me of where I had worshiped in Augusta. I liked that. It wasn't a tiny church, nor was it huge.

The choir sung some hymns and some upbeat gospel tunes. All of the pieces touched my heart. There wasn't any yelling or screaming but rocking and swaying. Though in the calmness, the Spirit was still there, and the congregation wasn't stiff and rigid. I was definitely a happy person.

The pastor got up and started speaking from 1 Corinthians 13:2, "Though I have the gift of prophecy, and understand all mysteries and all knowledge, and though I have all faith, so that I could remove mountains, but have not love, I am nothing." I realized that I hadn't been there for Laurel or Tad. And since there was no love for Dakari, being that he was irritating me, I couldn't have been his friend. That's not what I was about. When I don't have love, I can't feel for other people, and I am not happy with myself.

"Church, this morning I'll tell you that you've got to love God. Love Him, and He will give you the power to love anyone, including yourself. If you try to see the world through your own eyes, the injustices will make you so angry and so disappointed that you won't be able to carry on. In contrast, if you see your own problems and challenges through the Lord's eyes, then they won't seem like problems at all. They'll be little mountains that you must overcome. If you believe in Christ Jesus, He will give you the strength to overcome it. God will allow you to see every day as a great joy and journey."

That was my problem. I was seeing every day as something miserable. And though I remember my dad telling me on the first day of classes it would be a positive day, I wasn't seeing it that way. I wanted things my way. Since they weren't, I didn't want them at all. I never really thought about what God was doing. I never thought about His plan, only my own. I needed to know that He was in control and not me.

I needed to believe that. I needed to live that way. I needed to stay connected to people who were going to keep me on the right track. I needed to be in church, and I was so thankful that the Lord had led me to Double Springs.

Though I didn't know Reverend White nor any other members, what I felt made me feel like I needed to come back. In order to honor God with every area of my life, I needed the guidance of a local church. Though it had taken me a couple of times, I had found a home at Double Springs. I was no longer trying out churches.

7

Celebrating
What Exactly?

*W*e need to celebrate!" Tad said as he spun me around in the air outside the church.

"What are we celebrating?" I asked as we looked at the other people exiting the sanctuary.

They must have thought we were crazy. The unexpected twirl felt fun and free. It was weird. Why was he spinning me around? Why was he so happy?

When he opened my side of the car door, he said, "I just asked God to forgive me. I have not been giving God glory lately. I want to reflect who He is by obeying His Word. Now that's worth celebrating. I feel new."

He shut my car door and walked to the driver's side. It had been a good service, and I was happy that I had a place to come back to. Maybe that was it. Maybe Tad was happy that he had found a church home. During the altar call, Tad walked up to the pastor and prayed. Though I'd be coming back to Double Springs, I wasn't quite ready to say that this was going to be my official church home. It seemed better to just keep my membership in Augusta and visit here. Tad, on the other hand, thought differently.

"I've rededicated my life to Christ. I feel better than I've felt since I've come to school."

"What is rededication, really? I thought once you accept Christ, there is no going back? The Holy Spirit moves in and your life changes. Like it says in 2 Corinthians 5:17, we become a new creation."

All I saw Tad do was go up front and pray. I didn't know he was rededicating his life to the Lord. He was already a Christian. I was a little bit confused. I didn't want to say so, but my face showed that I didn't quite get it.

Tad replied, "You're right, Pay. If *true* repentance is there, when you cry out to God to save you, then He saves you once and for all. I never turned from God. My actions today were a mind thing, not a heart thing. Sorry if I confused you with my words. Another way to say it is, I recommitted to stay committed."

"Wow," I responded.

Tad said, "When I went to the front, I prayed to recommit myself as a Christian to God. To make Him first priority and remind myself that His Son died on the cross for me to save me from sin. He washed away old sins and hurts and all that stuff of the past. When I stay focused on Him, then I don't get all tangled up in wrong thinkin'. God says to seek first His kingdom and His righteousness. Then He will give us everything else we need. I feel good. I feel clean. My mind was so cloudy with all this football stuff and getting adjusted to my classes. Now my mind is on track. It feels good."

As we drove to the restaurant, I realized there it was again. Tad was growing closer to God, and I was stuck, stagnant in my old place. There was no way I could keep him accountable to anything. Pretty soon he wouldn't need me in his life. I would just be holding him back. We weren't on the same page.

How could he find me desirable when the things that consumed my mind weren't the same things that were exciting to him? I didn't know he had been struggling like I was, but now he had turned it around. If he hadn't totally done a 180-degree turn, at least he was close to that. Me? I didn't know where my life was going, but all I could do was be happy for him because he had made a commitment and planned to stick with it.

I couldn't get with that. That wasn't me. Yeah, I was happy for him, but how happy was I really? I guess deep down I wanted Tad to slip a little so that he could be more normal. So he could understand what I was going through. Not being such a "perfect Christian." I had thorns, and I needed someone to understand what that felt like. The service had touched me too, but now, in an instant, I'd slipped back into my funk.

Just as we pulled into a soul-food restaurant I said, "You know what? I'm kind of wiped out. Can we pass?"

"We're right here. It will only take a sec. You can go in for just a second?" Tad pleaded.

I knew he wanted to talk to me about this new feeling he had, but I didn't want to hear that. I just didn't know how to say it.

So I just simply said, "I'm sure I don't want to go in. I just wanna get back to my room."

He was disappointed. "Well, that's cool."

Later that week when I was studying for my psychology exam, I came across a picture of Tad and me at my debutante ball. We had had so much fun. I remember how happy I was that I had found him. The year had been so hard with my breakup with Dakari and all. Then, out of nowhere God allowed me to meet a good Christian guy, and I thought it was such a blessing.

It was such a blessing, but now, not even six months later, we were not even together. Now when Tad wanted to pour his heart out to me about the Lord, I didn't want to talk about it. I wondered why I was struggling in my walk with Christ. I knew I needed to call Tad. He had left me alone. There were no messages on my machine this whole week. Not that he owed me a call. I let him down in his time of need. I wanted to apologize.

"Hello, hello," the silly voice of Dakari answered.

I hadn't talked to him since he had gone out with my suite mate. Something must have happened, because she didn't come in gloating about their next date. I really hadn't given it much thought until I heard the jerk's voice.

"Hello," he said when he didn't hear a response from the other end.

Coldly I asked, "Is your roommate in?"

"Oh, so it's like that now? You're gonna call my room and not speak to me?"

"Yeah, Dakari, it's like that. Is Tad there?"

"No, he ain't here. I should just hang up since you can't speak to me."

"That's your prerogative."

"Dang! Why there gotta be all this hostility between me and you? You know my birthday's coming up next week. What are you going to get me?"

"Well, my birthday is the week after that. What are you gonna get me?" I asked, playing along.

"It depends on what I get."

I just chuckled. He was so silly. Even when I wanted to be angry at him, I couldn't be. He showed me that we could relate on a crazy level that both he and I understood.

"You're silly. What have you been up to?" I asked.

"Everything. I'm trying to continue with my role on the

team. The coach seems pretty happy."

"What about your grades, Dakari? Everything is not always about football. How are your grades?"

"Look, you didn't say you wanted specifics. You just asked me how things were going."

"OK, how about school? How about that?"

"It's cool. We've got tutors here. You know, tests from previous semesters to look at. I'm straight with that. I memorize the answers."

"Oh, what's up with that? You used to be a good student."

"It's different here. Back in high school it was kind of like we were getting a half education."

"Yeah, I feel you," I told him, completely understanding.

I took advanced placement classes, and this stuff was still hard for me. But I would never stoop so low as to cheat. It was good to know that when I defined myself, there were some things that I wouldn't do.

"Payton, on Sunday my brother's got a home game. My parents are gonna meet me at the Georgia Dome. Do you wanna ride down with me?"

I had never been to a professional football game before. Even though Drake wasn't my favorite person because I had heard him give Dakari props on trying to get with me, I was tired of Athens, and any diversion even for a little while was a chance I'd jump at.

"I'll go, but just as friends. Don't be misleading your mom and all that stuff."

"I know we are just friends. So are you sure you're coming?"

"Yeah. Do you know when Tad's coming back?"

"He went to church or something. We got out of practice a couple of hours ago, and he headed out to Bible study or somethin'. I don't know when he'll be back. He doesn't have to check in with me. I'll give him your message. I'll leave it on the desk for him. It'll be right beside the note that says what time I'm going to pick you up next week. I'm sure he'll see that."

"Why do you have to go there?"

"This is not about our date. I just wanna get under ole boy's skin! He's still been trippin', but it's in a different way. Now he ignores me and acts like he is better than me just because I don't get on my knees daily. I appreciate God and everything, but I work for my talent."

"Dakari, don't talk like that. It's a blessing from the Lord. That's why you are so talented."

"Yeah, it is a blessing, but I work hard for my talent. I'm thankful, but you can't be in the church and not in the gym expecting to be a great athlete. Faith without works is dead, right, church girl?"

I wanted to say, "And you can't be in the gym and not in the church and expecting to have great success either." But I knew I didn't want to go there with him; we would be debating all night. So I told him to give my message to Tad and then hung up the phone.

It was now Friday night, and Tad had not called me back. I wondered if Dakari had given him the message, and if Tad got the message maybe he thought I was beneath him, too, and didn't want to fool with me anymore. It took everything inside me to call once. And even though I wasn't going to call back, Tad was still on my mind.

"My son is eighteen and all that," Dakari's father said about Dakari as we were sitting in the Georgia Dome watching Drake play with the Falcons.

Dakari never told his parents that we were back together. I don't know why they went there and assumed that we were. Dakari nor I said a thing to change their minds, and I don't know why that was.

As I watched Dakari interact with his dad, I realized that he was not the guy that I wanted. He was so cocky, arrogant, and into himself. I needed a guy that could be into me, had confidence, but wasn't full of himself. Being "the man" is one thing, but knowing you're the man and feeling like no one can touch you is altogether unacceptable. And that was Dakari's world. I should have told him about himself, but I didn't.

But I could see where he got it from. When his brother, Drake, made a sack, you could see his arrogance out on the field. On the level that he was playing, in the NFL, when you accomplish something remarkable, you should celebrate, but what I witnessed was something much more. As I looked down at Hayli, who was going to be married in a year, there was something in her eyes that exuded sadness. She should be so happy and excited.

I wanted to talk to her, but I was no counselor. I couldn't help her out with whatever it was that she was going through. Plus, I was just a freshman in college. I was sure, if anything, she looked at me as a little sister, which wasn't too bad. She was too together to be worried with Drake, but I guess she loved him enough to look over that.

I didn't know what was wrong with her. As I thought about it, I hadn't seen her around campus. She was supposed to be in graduate school at Georgia.

"Let me trade places with you," I said to Mrs. Graham, since Hayli was on the other side of her.

"OK, y'all go ahead and have girl talk."

"Payton, how has school been?" Hayli asked, trying to spark up a conversation.

"Pretty overwhelming," I said, letting out a sigh.

"Yeah, it was like that for me. At least you've got a couple of friends there."

"Yeah, but how are you doing? You don't look like your

cheery old self. What's going on?"

Just as she was about to open up, Drake recovered a fumble and went down to the other end of the field for a touchdown.

"Go! Go!" she yelled matter-of-factly.

The crowd was screaming, and inside the Dome it sounded amplified. It was exciting. Especially when Drake scored. Now the Falcons were up by fourteen.

"Are you OK?" I asked. "I know we are not bosom buddies or anything, but I've always admired you. You seem so strong, so confident, and so sure of yourself, only in a good way. Your man just scored a touchdown, and you're not really into it. What's up?"

"You are sweet to care. I've just been doing a lot of praying."

I realized that I didn't know Hayli that well. I had never heard her talk about praying or the Lord before. I sensed that she needed to lean on someone, and I made my shoulder available.

She said, "I just feel like God wants me to cut back in some areas of my relationship. I'm engaged, and I want Him to bless our marriage, but how can I ask Him to bless our marriage if I'm not honoring Him with my actions while engaged? Things just aren't clicking for Drake and me. He wants to do one thing, and I want to do another. The other day, I went to his place, and I saw this girl leaving. This is the second time I'd seen this girl. I know I'm not crazy. Drake said she likes him, but he doesn't have any interest in her whatsoever. She had found where he lived and came to bring him something. It seemed like a suspect story, and I'm not about to marry a man that's gonna be out there. You know what I'm sayin', Payton?"

"Yes, I do," I told her honestly.

"I don't know what to do, but I've got time. We're not getting married until the off-season around Valentine's Day.

I'm not sure if I'm gonna make it to that day, at least not with Drake."

"Girl, you need to be sure," I told her. "But at least you are real with what's up. So many girls overlook all that stuff when their guy is making money. They just want to be someone's wife. Hayli, you have so much going for you. Why should you settle for what Drake is puttin' out? The right guy would see you as a treasure. Girl, you need to let Drake know what he has to lose. Maybe you should give him some space."

"How do you know all this stuff? For a freshman you might be ahead of the game."

We both laughed.

"But for real," I said, addressing her, "make sure he wants only you."

"Enough about me. What about you and Dakari? I thought I'd never see the two of y'all together. What's going on?"

"We're just friends, that's all. I just wanted to get out of Athens. Speaking of Athens, are you in school there?"

"I'm supposed to be, but I'm taking some classes at Georgia State."

"Wow! That's great."

"Yeah, but I'll be coming to Georgia every now and then. By the way, my friend Karlton, who replaced me on the cabinet, called me."

"Yeah, I know who you're talking about."

"He likes you. He definitely wants to get you involved with SGA. Are you familiar with it?"

"From what he told me, it sounds different from high school student government."

"It is. They have cabinet meetings, and they sit in with the student body president."

"Yes, I heard," I told her.

"Well, you need to get involved as a freshman, and

maybe you can be on the cabinet next year. Then maybe you can run for office yourself. Better start now. There's so much to get involved with in college, but most students don't take advantage of programs and extracurricular activities that could make them a more well-rounded individual. Don't you make that mistake. If SGA isn't your cup of tea, find out what is. Get involved with something."

We both smiled. I never had an older sister. I always wondered what it would be like. Dymond loved talking about hers. The bond they shared seemed really cool. If I had an older sister, I would want her to be like Hayli. Since that can't be changed, it was nice to have her in my life. She helped me with the stuff that no one thought about.

"Payton, when you want to get somewhere in life, there are steps you have to take. You don't just go from A to Z. If you want to get involved with SGA, get with Karlton. Let him groom you and show you the ropes."

We went to a restaurant in Norcross, Georgia, called Papadeaux. It was so good. I was always a seafood lover, and the fried catfish and alligator were delicious.

Around dessert time, the waiter came and brought a cake, and we all sang "Happy Birthday" to Dakari. His family then pulled out all of their presents. His brother gave him a fat envelope, and I knew it was nothing but cash. Dakari was so spoiled. He had the biggest smile upon his face.

"Payton, sweetie, I don't want you to think we forgot about you," his mom said as she pulled out a beautiful silver-wrapped box. "We've been celebrating your birthday ever since you and Dakari became friends. I know yours is next week. Here ya go, babe."

"It's beautiful," I said after opening it.

It was a gorgeous outfit from Saks.

"I'm so proud of all of you guys. We've got a wedding to plan, and soon there will be babies."

"Yeah, but those babies are a long way away," Hayli replied.

Mrs. Graham said, "Dakari got into Georgia and finally got some sense into his head and hooked back up with this lovely young lady. I'm so glad because I know that now that you are playing ball the girls are coming out of the woodworks."

"Mom!" He blushed.

"I know them girls. You better stick with one who has got something going on other than you. Stick with somebody who's about something. I don't need to say all that; look at y'all," Mrs. Graham replied.

"You better tell her," I mouthed to Dakari.

"Just leave it alone. We're celebrating," he whispered back.

"I don't want her to be celebrating us. There is no us."

"I know that, but as a birthday present to me, you can just keep your mouth shut."

"Whatever!"

He then reached over and kissed me on the cheek. He was just giving his parents what they wanted to see. Dakari would do what he could to please his parents so that he could get what he wanted. I'm sure it wasn't that big a deal. They would've been just fine with the fact that he wasn't dating me and we were just friends.

On the drive home, I bluntly asked him, "So what's with you? Why did you lie to your parents? I'm gonna tell your mama because I feel bad."

"Yeah, right, you feel bad. Like you're a saint."

"What's that supposed to mean?"

"Just what I said. You try to be with Tad, a good Christian boy, but why y'all ain't together now? More likely you've been lyin' more than you'd like to admit. And truthfully, Payton, it's not that bad. It's fun being young and not having any pressures. The church stuff is for folks my mom's age. It'll come along, but we're still young and kickin'

106

it. I care a lot about you because you're my girl. We've always been tight, but you need to go ahead and get over Tad. Y'all don't even click. It seems like as soon as y'all get close, and he starts doing all that preachin' stuff, you run right in the opposite direction. Who's in the opposite direction? Me. I'm just sayin', let's save ourselves some headache and drama, and let's have some fun."

"So what are you saying?" I asked for clarification. "Are you saying that you want to be with me?"

"Well, we can do that."

"You have been dating more girls than the days you have been here. Don't think I don't know."

"Well, I can stop all that when I get you. Did I miss the dorm?"

"The dorm is down that street."

"Oh, my bad. Think about it," he said as he let me out in front of my hall. "Don't I get a birthday kiss or something?"

"No, but for what it's worth, happy birthday."

"Oh, see . . . ya doin' a brother wrong."

"Look at you puttin' on makeup. I haven't seen that in a couple of days," I said as Laurel primped in the mirror.

"Have I been looking that bad?" she asked.

"Worse than that bad."

"Gymnastics practice has gotten me so beat up. I'm just trying to make the team. I'm just so stressed. This morning I feel good."

"Really? Why?"

"Because it's your birthday!"

"You remembered," I said to her.

She pulled a cutely wrapped box out of the closet. I was overjoyed to find perfume inside. It was something I really needed.

"Eighteen? Are you excited?"

"Laurel, I've been waiting for eighteen for a long while, so I can have some sense of independence, but now that it's here, I don't know how I feel."

"Yeah, I understand. I felt that way this summer when I turned eighteen."

"When is yours?"

"The fourth of July. People always have a good time on my birthday."

"Well, October fourth is not a holiday at all."

"Yes, it is. It's your birthday."

"Yeah, how did you know, anyway?"

"I spoke to your mom a couple of weeks ago, and she told me. She also told me to give you this."

Laurel pulled a big box from under some blankets in the closet. It was a brand-new CD player and quite a few CDs that my brother, Perry, had picked out. He and I like the same music, so I was excited about the new songs. Also in the box were clothes and shoes. No wonder my mother didn't want to take me shopping in August when I had asked her. This was a nice surprise.

"Thanks, Laurel."

"You know it was hard hiding it from you," Laurel confessed. "Every time you went in the closet I thought you were about to ask what that big box was."

"I didn't see a box."

"I thought you would see it under that big blanket."

"I wasn't really paying attention. It was really nice of you to keep my mom's secret. Last year they forgot."

"They forgot your birthday?"

"Well, kind of. With all the other things they were shelling out money for, like graduation, prom, and the debutante ball . . . "

"Debutante ball? What's that?"

"I'll have to tell you later, but to give you the short version it's when girls are introduced to society. It's very nice. I'll have to show you the tape."

"I'd like to see that."

"Well, let me get to class."

"Wait," Laurel said with a look of disgust. "Are you wearing that?"

"What? What's wrong with this? You wear sweats to class every day."

"I know but you were just talking about how I looked bad. Payton, at least fix your face and your hair. I don't know that much about black hair, but that looks mangled. It's your birthday . . . dress up!"

"Well, I look like a slob because I feel like one. See ya," I mumbled as I shut the door. Quickly I turned my key and reopened it. "Thanks for the present."

As I sat in psychology, I wondered what my grade was going to be in the class. Cammie was a little disappointed because she had gotten a C, but I would be happy to get a C. I thought the midterm exam a couple of days ago was extremely hard. My heart sank when I turned over my paper and saw I had a flag waving at me.

Cammie said, "What did you get?"

Embarrassed, I answered, "I can't believe this."

She saw the disappointment in my eyes, and I'm sure she figured it out. She turned around.

"I've never gotten this grade before. Ever."

I don't know why I was that surprised because when I took the test, I had no answer for half of the questions. I'd studied but maybe not enough. Dakari was right. The academics were much higher in college.

"Well," I spoke in a whisper, "I've just got to do better."

Later that day, I finally made it back to my room. It had been such a hectic day. I had tons of homework and a bad grade. Life was getting tough.

"Look at this," Laurel exclaimed as I entered the room. "Eighteen roses. Three different colors. They are so beautiful. I've been dying for you to get here and open the card. Who do you think they're from?"

"They're probably from my dad."

However, to my surprise they were from Dakari. *Don't think I forgot about our conversation. Although you wouldn't make my day with a kiss, I hope this makes yours.*

"Those are from Dakari?" Jewels said as she peeked her head in, "How dare he send you flowers!"

It was my birthday, and she had been a brat since the day we'd arrived. I wasn't going to allow it any longer. She had to be told.

"Don't be comin' up in here showin' your insecurities. Dakari was my boyfriend for three years. He loved me, and he knows he made a mistake at one time, but now he wants me back. Jewels, the date you guys had didn't work out. It's not my fault. So get over it and get the heck out of my room."

"Proudly," she said as she threw a present onto my bed.

For a moment I felt horrible. Here she was giving me a present, and I was telling her off. Then, I picked it up and noticed it was from Tad, and all the guilt was removed.

"It's from Tad," Laurel exclaimed with so much joy you would think it was her present. "Open it."

"It feels like a book," I said to her.

"Well, open it anyway."

Sure enough, it was a book. It was a Christian nonfiction novel by Priscilla Evans Shirer called *A Jewel in His Crown*.

When I opened it, the title page read:

To my dear Payton,

Though things haven't worked out the way I'd like them to, I still think the world of you. I think of you

110

AS A VERY PRECIOUS JEWEL IN GOD'S CROWN. YOU ARE
WORTH MORE THAN THE MOST EXPENSIVE DIAMOND YOU
COULD EVER THINK OF.
HAPPY BIRTHDAY.

TAD

Laurel had read over my shoulder, and she screamed, "That's so sweet! What are you gonna do? Are you gonna go out with Tad or Dakari?"

"I'm tired. I don't feel like going anywhere."

"We've got to celebrate!"

As I looked into her words, I appreciated them. Yet, there didn't seem any reason for me to celebrate. I couldn't celebrate my F. I couldn't celebrate that I had two guys that liked me but didn't really like me. I couldn't celebrate the fact that my suite mate disgusted me or the fact that I missed home.

Frustrated, I babbled, "Laurel, my life isn't the greatest right now. So I have to ask . . . we'd be celebrating what exactly?"

8

Deciding to Quit

"Here, you're supposed to pass this out," our suite mate Anna, dashed into my room and said as she handed me a bunch of papers.

"What's this? What's this for? What's this about?" I drilled her.

"It's the most horrible thing. One of the girls who lives on the third floor—her name is Worth Zachary—do you know her?"

"No."

"She's missing."

"What do you mean she's missing?"

"She went out. They assume on a date . . . and she never came back," Anna explained.

Laurel came to the room, overhearing the last part and said, "Oh, my gosh, I just heard about that. This is awful. What do we need to do? Pass out flyers?"

Anna replied, "Yeah, I just gave some to Payton. I'm going to head out to the campus grounds to hand them out.

You guys can come with me if you want."

"Like *you* can find somebody," Jewels cut in from the bathroom. "Anna, you don't know the difference from your left and right. How are you going to find somebody? You are so worthless."

"Well, I'm going to try. I'm going to do everything that I can," Anna defended, practically in tears, scooting by Laurel, which was hard because Anna was kind of wide.

"She is such a crybaby," Jewels said. "I am so glad that she didn't get into our sorority. She would've brought our popularity down. Even as far as a roommate is concerned . . . Payton, I should have taken you over her."

"Jewels, you don't even have to entertain that thought, because, if I had to room with you, you would have had the room to yourself."

I thought, *I'd rather be dead than room with her.*

I know it sounded harsh, but Jewels was crazy. That chick took the cake from all the folks I knew back home. Starr, her cousin Summer, even my cousin Pillar. Jewels was just plain crazy. It was her way or no way. It was her world or no one's world. It was so messed up that she was so full of herself. Jewels thought she was the only one good at anything.

She liked Laurel a lot, and they were hanging out a little bit. I didn't know what was going on, and, frankly, I didn't care. Deep down I knew Laurel needed to watch her back, because Jewels was only in relationships for what she could get out of them.

"We're trying to find Worth Zachary! Has anybody seen Worth Zachary?" I yelled across the open area of the campus grounds as I handed out flyers.

"She's in one of my classes. She's missing?" a strange girl

113

said to me.

"Yeah, it's been a couple of days now."

"I'll be on the lookout. This is so terrible. My roommate and I saw a couple of strange guys looking in our window."

"Are you serious?" I questioned her, getting a funny feeling in my stomach.

"Yeah! We've all just got to be careful and watch out for one another."

"Yep, you never can be too careful," I added.

We went our separate ways, and I continued handing out flyers until I had passed them all out.

It was Wednesday, and I had a big test in two days. I knew it was suicide not to apply myself. Studying was the last thing on my mind. What did I expect? For the material to miraculously fly into my brain cells? There was no chance of that happening. I just didn't feel like studying. I was weighed down with so many things. I actually hated my new surroundings. Maybe subconsciously I didn't want to do well.

Sure enough, when Friday came, and I was in my math class, I didn't understand one equation. My eyes were puffy, but I knew it was no time to be sad. I had brought this on myself. I had made my bed, and now I had to lie in it. In fact, I had a paper to write in literature, and I hadn't even read the book. How was I supposed to write a paper on a book that I hadn't even read? This was so against what I was used to. I was a good student at home, but now I wasn't even applying myself. On those rare occasions when I did study, it would be a little too late.

However, the next week when I got my literature paper back and saw that big red flag, I knew I had to do something. Otherwise, I would be back in Augusta, the place I was missing. Though I wanted to go home, I didn't want to be there because I flunked out of UGA. I only wanted to go home for vacations, but nothing in me was allowing me to turn my study habits around.

———————————

"Dad? What are you doing here?" I asked as my dad came up to my dorm and surprised me.

"Your brother is out in the car. We just came up to go to the big game with you."

Good thing I didn't have a life because I could have been going to the game with my friends. Since I was so in between Tad and Dakari, I wasn't too hyped to go and see them play. However, I might as well go with my dad because I wasn't doing anything else. I needed to study, but going to the game would be a great diversion from that.

When the dorm director had come to the door and said my dad was up front, I couldn't believe it. I thought, *There is no way that Dad is up front. This is Saturday, the busiest day at the car lot.*

"I know you told me you were coming, but you never leave the dealership on Saturday. So why is that changing?" I asked my father.

"Well, I realize that I only have two kids, and you guys are growing up. This gave Perry and me a chance to talk, and he misses his big sister just as much as your mom and I do."

"Did Mom come?"

"No, she wanted to, but she had a sorority meeting."

My mom had just gotten appointed to a big position in her sorority, Delta Sigma Theta. The new regional director had named her state coordinator. Mom had always been active with her chapter, but I was sure she was going to step it up a notch because she had been making her rounds to all the other chapters. With my mom at the head of anything, she always wanted to make sure it was the best. So I knew my mom would want Georgia to have the best Deltas around.

"Come here, girl. Give your dad a hug. I really do miss you. You're looking kind of tired. What have you been doing? Sleeping or studying hard?"

I didn't want to lie to my father because I knew he'd see straight through me if I did. Studying was no joke. However, I couldn't tell him that either.

"Sleeping," I told him honestly.

Before I could reach to hug him, he pulled me to him. It was a tight embrace—one that I had not had in a long time from my dad. He had hugged me at graduation and told me he was proud. He'd also told me I was beautiful the night of the debutante ball. This hug was different. I could tell he really missed me.

I got kind of embarrassed when people in the dorm passed by and looked at us in a weird way. I shouldn't care, but it was strange. There I was standing in the lobby hugging this old man. They didn't know he was my dad; they could've been thinking anything. He was my dad, so I didn't care what they thought. I got the insecurities out of my mind and hugged him back because I missed him, too. The fact that he drove all the way up here to see me might make it a better day than I had had in a while.

Clowning with Perry and my dad at the game was better than I could have ever imagined. We yelled and screamed, ate hot dogs, and just enjoyed being a family. It was easy to feel good about myself knowing that I had people in my life who cared about me. I wasn't the only one who thought I could be someone, do something, or go somewhere with my life. Being with them in a crowd of seventy-thousand-plus let me know that I was just as special as any of those football players on the field.

Georgia was up fifteen points, and this was the day we were playing the Florida Gators. I hadn't even thought about going to the game. Jett Phillips, the Florida player I knew, had given me his home info, but I had never called him. At the time, I didn't know what my dorm number would be, so I never gave him a way to get in touch with me. But there he was on the field and down by fifteen points. He quickly led Florida on a scoring drive that was amazing. He threw an eighty-nine-yard touchdown pass. Everyone thought we were crazy when my dad, Perry, and I stood up and cheered for him. I wanted the Gators to lose, but I still wanted Jett to do well.

"Your boy is all that. What? What? We're excited because we know him," my brother said to the people staring at us.

"Sit down and watch the game. Who cares what people think? They didn't buy my ticket to get in here," my dad joked, being his silly self.

On the next drive for the Bulldogs, the ball was given to the running back, Randall Hope. As soon as the quarterback gave him the ball, a defensive lineman for the Gators came and stripped it. It was a horrific sight. The fans were sick.

"See that? That's why Tad needs to be in there," Perry said.

"For real," my dad added.

Jett was back on the field. I must admit that not even I thought he could hit another long ball like he did on the last drive. That time instead of a pass for eighty-nine yards, he hit one for ninety-three.

"He's Heisman bound," my dad said in awe.

Now the people around me were really tripping. We were going to lose the game. To stay in the play-off hunt, we needed to win. We wanted to go to a big-bowl appearance. We were undefeated, but at this point so was Florida.

Now the game was tied forty-one to forty-one. Unfortunately, there were only three minutes left on the clock, but we had the ball. Now it was time to move it and score.

I was never this big a football fan. High school was OK, but this was a whole different level. This game was shown nationwide. Laurel and her family were here somewhere, but we weren't really hanging that tight anymore. I just hoped that wherever they were, they were having fun.

"I hope they don't hand it to that running back," my dad told me as he saw Randall running onto the field.

On the first down the ball was given back to Randall, and even though I saw it, I didn't believe it. The ball in his hand ended up on the ground, and we didn't recover it. Florida did. There were now two minutes and thirty seconds left on the clock. If defense could hold them, we would go into overtime.

Jett's first two passes were incomplete. It was now third and ten. He dropped back, threw it to the receiver over the middle, and picked up the first down. The next play, he threw it to the left side and picked up twenty-five yards.

The clock was still running, and Florida was working it. The next thing we knew, the Gators were in a position to kick a field goal, and when they did it, the time ticked off the clock, and it was as if every Georgia player could have died. We had lost the big game.

"Playing Florida for homecoming was just stupid," my dad said. "You know that was going to be all-out war. Oh, well, it's over."

As we headed to the car, we ran into Laurel and her family.

"Payton! Payton!" she said to me.

"Hi there, Payton," Reverend Shadrach greeted me. "I hear things are going well for you and Laurel as roommates. We've been praying for y'all."

"Sir, this is my father, Mr. Skky. Dad, this is my roommate, Laurel, and her family."

After we introduced our families, Laurel pulled me aside and asked, "Are you going to go say hi to Jett?"

The thought never crossed my mind. I didn't even know how to find him. Even if I found him, I didn't know if he'd want to stop and chat.

"When they get back on the bus, you can at least wave. If he sees you, then he'll come and say something. I want to meet him, Payton. He did so good today. We lost, and I'm not happy, but I'm a huge fan of Jett's."

"OK, let's try and do that. Dad, can we wait until Florida comes out?"

"Yeah, Dad, maybe we can see Jett," my brother added. "Do you think he remembers us?"

"I don't know, but he will probably remember Payton."

"Ha, ha, ha," I said to my dad. "Very funny."

Finally the Gators came out. They had a lot of fans up here in Athens to cheer them on. Perry and Laurel's middle brother, Lance, had moved themselves to the front of the crowd so that they could yell out to get Jett's attention. I didn't think they'd be very successful at that. Surely he'd be too busy to stop and talk.

But after about five minutes, they called me, "Payton, come on! We got him!"

Laurel grabbed my hand and pulled me to the front of the crowd.

"Hey, Payton!" Jett said as though I was a very good friend.

I was happy to know that we still shared the connection we had on the cruise ship. He spoke to my dad and Perry, and I introduced him to Laurel and her family, and he reached out to hug me.

"The star of the game," he said. "Did you see me? I took your advice and put it all on Jesus Christ. It seems that when I do, I do extremely well in the game. How are things for you up here at UGA?"

"I'm adjusting. Do you have a pen? We need to exchange numbers."

"That would be great, but I don't have anything to write on."

"Here, I've got something," Laurel announced helpfully.

It was great to see Jett, and I was glad the Lord was blessing him. We said we would keep in touch, and as I walked in a different direction from him, I felt we would.

It was one of those mornings when I just didn't want to get up. The thought of resting comfortably in a grave seemed more appealing than getting out on this crisp day and going to class. I looked over at Laurel's bed and saw it was already made. She must have gotten an early start. I hoped her day would be great, and if mine ever got started, I hoped it would be great as well.

No sooner than I thought of Laurel did she enter the room. Her somber mood frightened me.

"Laurel, what's wrong?"

"They found Worth Zachary. Payton, they found her twenty minutes down the road. They found her in a Dumpster at an abandoned gas station."

"Is she OK?"

"No, Payton. She's dead."

My heart dropped to the ground as if it were a glass that had shattered into a hundred pieces. I didn't want it to be true. I didn't know Worth, but she'd lived on the third floor. She was a freshman just like me, and now she was gone.

"They don't want us to go to class today," Laurel said. "They've got some counselors coming to talk about it, but I don't want to talk about this. What is there to say?"

I went over to hug her and give her comfort.

"Is it mandatory that we go to counseling?"

"Yeah, that's what I've been told. I don't even know how you could sleep. Look out of the window. It's a zoo out there with all the media. We need to get dressed. We have a meeting in fifteen minutes."

I was spoiled, and I realized that during my stay at UGA. At home, I'd shared a bathroom with my brother. Fortunately, he didn't do a lot of primping. He was in and out and was never in my way. After sharing a bathroom with three females, who have to blow-dry their hair, I became sick and tired of waiting. Then, when I finally got into the bathroom, I was always stepping on strands of either brunette, blonde, or red hair.

Knocking softly I said, "Laurel told me that we have a meeting. Could y'all please hurry up?"

"If Anna would get out of my way so that I can make my face even more beautiful, then you can have the sink," Jewels said snobbishly.

"Whatever, Jewels. Just hurry up."

Anna opened the door and said, "I'm finished, Payton."

"You did all that for . . . what exactly? You still look ugly," Jewels said to Anna with a dirty smirk on her face.

I had heard Jewels go off on this poor girl quite a bit, but that was their business. I didn't want to share a bathroom with Jewels, nor her with me, so I gave her a look to tell her not to start with me. She was annoyed, but so was I. After hearing the news about Worth, the day was shaping up to be horrible.

As I stepped into the eerie hall, I wondered, *Why, Lord? Worth was so young and beautiful.* I heard she was an only child as well, so I knew her parents were absolutely devastated.

"Such a tragedy," I mumbled to myself. "I hope she knew You, Lord."

This was so depressing. More than fifty girls, mostly freshmen, had squeezed in the commons area of the dorm to talk with counselors about the death of one of our own. It wasn't supposed to be like this. These first few months were supposed to be filled with joy. Even without knowing Worth, a part of me was gone. A part that held the naive notion that this was a safe place had to change. Clearly, nothing could be taken for granted.

The counselor began, "I'm sure that by now all of you know why we are here. It is with deep regret that I'm here to mediate this occasion. Sometimes when things like this happen, it helps to talk through them. First I want to start by asking does everybody know the details of this incident?"

Most girls shook their heads, no. I didn't want to know. Probably because I wouldn't be able to get it out of my head. I'd more than likely think about it over and over and imagine it were me in her situation.

"Because it was an unsafe accident, one that we felt could've been prevented, we must talk about it. Not to frighten or upset you but to make you wiser women. A while ago, your fellow dorm mate went on a date with a stranger. You don't have to be alarmed; the gentleman is in custody. Though he is thirty-two, he looks fairly young. Based on the district attorney's case, it looks like this guy tried to date her. She thought he was a college student, but she did not know for sure. No one knew where she went, not her parents or even her roommate. She just left with a strange man. I don't want to insinuate that she was asking for it, wanting to go out and be killed, raped, or assaulted, but when you don't take extra precautions, anything is possible. A great date may be one you'll never recover from, and that's what happened in this case," the counselor told us.

We were still. Every word was eerie. I hated that this truly happened.

The counselor stated, "The gentleman in custody is suicidal. He's never killed anyone before, but he's tried to kill himself several times. He was a good actor, but, ladies, I have to warn you, don't be fooled by good lines."

Instantly, I thought back to the beginning of the year when I had gone out with Karlton. As the man just said, my night went great, but it could've been tragic. Somewhere along the way, I had gotten enough sense to call Laurel and leave a message on her machine, letting her know where I was and who I was with. I wasn't thinking smart when I left the dorm that night, but somewhere along the way I realized that I needed to take care of myself. I had to find out about someone before I hopped in a car. I couldn't share this story with Worth. For her, it was too late. I could do nothing about the past. Worth was gone. However, there were several girls in front of me that needed to hear my story. They needed to hear that though I wasn't smart, I turned it around.

So I said, "Yeah, y'all listen to him. That happened to me." I went on to explain.

Several other girls talked about how dates they went on in the last couple of weeks turned sour. Several admitted that they never let anyone know where they were going and were so thankful that they weren't in Worth's place. Talking about it was good, and I appreciated the counselor's taking time out to understand our pain.

The counselor closed, "You've got to be wise and take care of yourselves and watch out for one another. When you get involved with the wrong person, it only takes one time for you not to be able to change things. If you get with a person who cares nothing about his life, then it's no big deal for him to take yours. This incident is horrible, but if what happened to Miss Zachary can help any one of you not fall prey to the same thing, then in death she has given you all an awesome gift. I pray all of you girls possess wisdom that will enable you to always be careful."

"That was a real classic touch, Payton," Tad said to me over the telephone.

I had written him a note to thank him for my birthday

present. I sent Dakari one as well, but I hadn't heard from him. He probably didn't even open the card. It's not like I expected anything different from Mr. Graham.

"Oh, you got the card?"

"Yeah, it was sweet. It smelled good, too. I really appreciated it."

"Not as much as I appreciated the book," I responded.

"Well, I meant every sweet word."

"As soon as I finish all of my required reading, I plan to dive in and be blessed."

"Well, that was my hope in picking it out for you. Finding a gift for a lady who has got everything is hard."

"I do not have everything."

"You do, too," he said, mocking me back in a cute way. "But no matter how much material you have about Christ, you can never get enough."

I needed to make reading *A Jewel in His Crown* a priority, because lately I sure didn't feel like a jewel. I was glad I had Tad. His mission was to be my brother in Christ.

"I see in the last couple of games that the running back has been fumbling the ball. They need to put you in the game!"

Tad laughed in a smooth way. "Thanks. Hopefully I'll get some playing time soon."

We ended the conversation in a nice way, wishing each other the best. After I had hung up the phone, my heart dropped. I felt like I had let a good one go. However, I was thankful that we were still together to talk about the most important thing: Jesus Christ. Who knows, maybe if I kept growing . . . Well, I've just got to keep growing.

Later that night, I was in my room resting. Well, I was trying to rest. I couldn't because I heard Jewels going off on Anna in the bathroom.

"Can't you get out of here! You're in my way, you fat pig! I'm trying to get ready. Me and Laurel are going to a formal dance, but you're not an Alpha Gamma, so you can't go. Use the bathroom later!"

I wanted to go and tell her, "Girl, shut up. You are not all that." But just a while back Anna didn't even want me as her suite mate, so now she had to stand up for herself. Again, that was between them. I just wished they would settle down so that I could get some sleep.

Laurel had made friends with a girl on the second floor who was also in her sorority. Laurel decided to go up to her room to get ready. I guess they were going to bond. I was glad that she was making good friends because I knew she couldn't be tight with Jewels. Jewels was crazy.

"What are you staring at, Anna? You could never look like this. Looking at me isn't going to make my looks rub off on you. Sorry, but you're out of luck."

Why in the world was Anna putting up with that mess? She wasn't saying anything back. I couldn't see her face, but I was sure after all that rejection, she had to be sad.

Though I was starting to feel sorry for Anna, that still wasn't my problem. I heard fidgeting at my door, and then in walked Laurel. She was so beautiful in her peach satin gown.

"Payton, I just wanted you to see me. Are you asleep?" she called softly.

I jumped out of bed. "No, no. I wanted to see you."

"How do I look?"

"Beautiful," I told her honestly. "You look good."

"Well, I bet she doesn't look this good," Jewels said as she walked inside the room wearing a stunning silver fitted gown. She just wanted us to see her and then she stepped back into the bathroom and continued primping.

"Don't even get sad," I told Laurel as I saw the smile on her face turn downward. "You've got it goin' on. Don't let Jewels trip on you. She's been talking craziness to Anna all night. Do you have a date?"

"I'm going with one of the frat boys. I know all about him. He's really nice."

"Good. It should be fun. Enjoy yourself."

Two hours had passed, and I was still in my long johns lying in the bed. I had planned to take a bath after Laurel left, but Anna was finally getting her time in the bathroom. I didn't want to disturb her. Thirty minutes later, I noticed water was running. In my daze I didn't pay it any mind. However, when I glanced at my clock twenty minutes later, it was still running.

When I stepped out of bed to go check on Anna, my carpet was damp. I quickly rushed to the door and saw water coming from the bottom of it. Turning the doorknob, I was frightened to find it was locked.

I banged on the door. "Anna! Anna, it's me, Payton! Open the door! Are you OK?"

There was no response, and the water was still running. I dashed out of my room and went to where the dorm director stayed.

"Something's not right! Something's wrong with Anna!" I yelled hysterically.

Less than two minutes later she was unlocking my bathroom door. My mouth hung open as I was stopped in my tracks to find Anna laid out in the tub with an empty pill bottle swimming in the water.

"Call 911, Payton."

I still couldn't move. What was happening? I couldn't move.

"Call 911!" the dorm director said louder. "Move, Payton; go now!"

I hurried over to the phone and dialed 911. I was scared. *Father, please help her. Lord, I don't even think she knows You. Lord, please.*

I went to direct the emergency crew to my room. They tried desperately to revive Anna and with each attempt, they were unsuccessful.

God, did You hear me? You have got to send a miracle. Don't let her be successful in deciding to quit.

9

Becoming
Someone Else

The paramedics revived her all of a sudden. Anna was back! She wasn't totally out of the woods, but she was breathing.

"Pay . . . ton? What's . . . going on? What's going on?" Anna asked groggily.

"It'll be OK," I told her as we connected. "It'll be OK."

"No, I just remember feeling really bad. I felt like I didn't matter and like I didn't want to be here."

"No, don't talk like that," I cut in.

"No, I've . . . got to tell you, Payton. I just didn't . . . want to go on. It was easy to imagine . . . not being here. It seemed . . . the world would be perfect without me."

"You can't think like that," I said as I got the strength to speak wiser than my years. "Who cares what Jewels thinks? What the heck does she know?"

As I said those words to Anna, I felt as if I had let her down. I had heard Jewels say all of those horrible things to Anna, and I hadn't intervened. Jewels had verbally abused her for a couple months, and I had just kept to myself. *It's not my problem,* I had said to myself over and over. *Let someone else handle it,* I'd rationalized. That was wrong. I should have been the someone else to stop it.

"Yeah, Jewels hurt me . . . but this started way before Jewels. I have always been made fun of. I just thought by killing myself I would have been doing everybody a favor."

"Please don't talk like that. You don't mean that."

The emergency worker said to me, "She is really weak. We have to take her in. She needs to rest. We need you to help us keep her calm so that we can take her in. She's not all the way out of the woods yet."

"Anna," I said as I bent down to the stretcher, "I want you to save your energy, OK?"

"Payton, I don't feel good," she called out.

"They're going to make you feel better. You're going to be OK," I said, unable to hold back the tears any longer.

As I watched them roll her out, not only did the tears come, but they came crashing down like a waterfall. I was devastated as I actually felt Anna's pain. The whole semester I wanted to be someone other than who I was. I just didn't feel as though I measured up to the other girls at Georgia. I actually had self-esteem issues. Thankfully, I had never felt the need to take my own life. Though wanting to be someone else isn't good, wanting to die is even worse.

Ephesians 2:10 says that we were all created as His workmanship. God created us after His own image. Each and every one of us has a purpose. He has a plan for our lives. But if we kill ourselves now, how will we live out His plan? The next chance I got, I was going to tell Anna this, and in my moments of gloom I was going to remind myself. It gets dark sometimes, but we have to hold on and get through it. God helps us get through all the tough stuff.

Different girls from the dorm, whom I did not know, were helping to clean up the room. Jewels and Laurel had no idea. They were dancing the night away, and I was glad that they were not there. Seeing Anna in the tub breathless and blue was a sight that I would never forget. Although we didn't click, and I didn't comfort her until tonight, I was still thankful that the Lord used me to help save her life.

"Thank You, Lord," I cried out. "Thank You!"

I didn't know if the girls in my room were Christians or not, and I really didn't care. At that moment it was just me and God.

The praises kept coming and the tears kept flowing. I was crying out because I was hurting. All of a sudden I felt arms around me. Cammie had come to help. She saw me in anguish.

"Your knees are soaked," Cammie said to me.

"I don't care. I just don't care," I said, making no sense.

I knew God understood me. The wet knees were insignificant. With what I had just gone through, I knew Jesus was there. If I had to kneel on the bottom of a twelve-foot pool to praise God, I would do it. I just had to praise Him.

Cammie insisted, "Payton, go to my room, get changed, and rest. You've been through a lot. Don't try to be strong and handle this all by yourself. Let me be your friend and help you through this."

I mouthed the words "thank you" as she helped me up. She grabbed a few of my things and took me up to her room.

A week before, my dad had stood in the hallway hugging me as people looked at us. This time, on that horrible night when I had seen my suite mate try to take her own life, I was even happier to see my father.

"How did you know, Dad? How did you get here so quickly?"

"The school has some type of policy to call parents when dramatic things happen. Your mom and I want you to come home tonight."

"I'll be home next weekend for Lucy Laney's homecoming."

"Well, we want you to come home tonight so that you can rest properly. You don't need to be here tonight."

Laurel wasn't back from the dance, and I hated leaving a note telling her all the details. I know that wasn't how I would want to find out. Even as I went back to my room to get some clothes, I felt sick. So surely, maybe just for that night, I didn't need to stay.

Since I knew I was in the company of my father, the sleep that was impossible to get in Cammie's room came easy as we drove back home to Augusta.

My dad stroked my face and said, "OK, babe, we're home."

Home, the safe place where I so desperately wanted to be. Perry and Mom were waiting up for me. Mom had some freshly baked, chocolate chip cookies. She also had a glass of milk waiting.

"Hey, honey," she said with her arms wide open.

"Oh, Mom."

"Sweetie, it's OK," she said as I broke down into sobs. "Your dad told me your suite mate was OK."

"Yeah, she had to get her stomach pumped, and now she's stable."

"Have your cookies while I run you a nice hot bath so you can get some rest."

My mom was taking care of me, and it was great. We hadn't had one of our talks in a long time, but it was good when we did because she was the best mom. Her sweet gestures at that moment proved that to be true.

While soaking in the tub, I thought of the day's events. I still couldn't believe it. God had used me to save someone's life. It was so ironic because as a Christian, God calls us to share His words so He can save souls. However, I don't witness enough, and I don't tell enough people about God. It's probably because my life isn't the best example. As my cousin once told me, "How can I serve the same God you serve when you have so many issues?" If I believed in God the way I said I do, I should have more faith.

Help me, Lord, to change my thoughts. Help me to concentrate more on You than I do on me. Thanks for using me, despite my actions. I want to be worthy of Your grace. Most of all, Lord, help me to grow in Your Word and help me to learn to enjoy it.

It was now about three in the morning, and I found myself tossing and turning. I just couldn't sleep. I just kept thinking about the day's events. What if I would've gotten up sooner? What if I would've stepped in all those times Jewels was being so cruel? Before I could get too down on myself, I thought, *What if I hadn't gotten up at all? Thank goodness that I did.*

My phone rang.

"It's three in the morning. Who could be calling Perry this late?" I said, grabbing the phone, trying to be nosy.

"Payton?"

"Laurel, you got my note."

"Yeah, thanks for leaving it. I can't believe this is happening."

"Laurel, where are you? Are you staying in the room?"

"Yeah, they cleaned it up. You can't even tell anything happened. You won't believe this."

"What?" I asked her.

"Jewels cried."

"She should be crying. She's such a stupid jerk."

"I hear you're a hero."

"No, I was just lying here feeling guilty because I heard the water running, and I didn't get up until it was almost too late."

"But it wasn't too late. It's OK to be a hero. I just wish I would've been there," Laurel comforted.

"Well, I'm glad you weren't because the thought of seeing her like that . . . "

"Yeah, you don't have to explain. I'm sure it was awful."

"It really was."

"You know, Payton, I have to admit that I had heard Jewels go off on Anna quite a bit. I just wasn't bold enough to tell Jewels that she was wrong. When Jewels was crying tonight, I told her that she was mean. I also told her about Jesus Christ and how He forgives. She still didn't want to hear it, but I think I'm starting to break through."

"That's good. You've got to pray for me because I can't stand Jewels right now. If I saw her, there's no telling what I would do."

"Payton . . . "

"No, I'm serious."

"When are you coming back?"

"Tomorrow, but then I will be back down here next weekend."

"I didn't mean to call you this late. I just wanted to make sure you were OK. I'm praying for you, Payton."

"Please do, Laurel. I know He's going to be the only way for me to get through this."

"Amen."

"On a brighter note, how was the dance?"

"It was eventful, and I had a lot of fun," Laurel expressed with slight glee.

"Thanks for checkin' up on me."

"Yeah, no problem."

The next week went by so fast. Anna hadn't come back to school yet, but I was able to sleep in my room again.

Laurel was right; you couldn't tell anything had happened. I had asked the Lord to take away the bad memories, and every time I prayed, I was able to get a good night's sleep.

It was now Friday, and I was at Lucy Laney's homecoming.

"Payton Skky."

Who is that? I thought to myself as I turned around. I should have known. It was none other than Starr Love.

"Starr, why aren't you at school somewhere?"

"I took a year off."

That figured—she was always trying to live off of her dad.

"Have you seen my cousin Summer at school? I've been up there to visit, and I haven't run into you. Are you sure that you're at UGA?"

I had forgotten that Summer was at UGA doing gymnastics. I needed to ask Laurel if she knew her.

"She's trying to make the gymnastics team. She's up against some white girl. Summer is better than her, so I'm sure she'll make it. Every time I go up there, I ask has she seen you, and she always says no."

I was hearing Starr talk, but I was thinking about Laurel. Summer was probably the girl Laurel was trying to beat for the team. She never told me she was black, but Laurel would never categorize or describe someone's abilities by the color of his or her skin.

"Well, I just saw you give your crown away. Now you are just like me . . . nobody's homecoming queen."

"But we will never be alike because I was a homecoming queen. Were you?"

"Whatever, Payton," she said as she brushed me aside. "When I go back up to UGA, I don't think I will be looking you up. I think I will just find Dakari and Tad, and we will have a good time together. Just the three of us."

"Do whatever, but it'll take a miracle to get them around you."

Starr rolled her eyes and stormed off. I knew I shouldn't have gone off on her, but it just felt so good. Then I thought about how Jesus wouldn't approve. I was acting no better than Jewels. I vowed to handle it another way next time.

Before I left the game, I ran into one of my old teachers. She went on to tell me that my dad told her of the recent events. She had seen him at the dealership when she purchased a car.

"You've been on my mind because you were one of my best students. You are such a pretty, sweet girl. You just need to stay encouraged. I know things get tough, but always trust God that He has an awesome plan for your life. Always do your best. Use the skills He's given you with all your heart. Do that, and you will be as successful at UGA as you were here. I know it's a big pond up there."

"Yeah."

"But regardless, a big pond or a small pond, a big fish or a little fish, being able to swim is the only thing that matters."

I pondered on that for a minute and thought, *I've got to stop sinking and start swimming.*

I hugged her and thanked God for sending her my way to remind me that I needed to keep trusting Him and quit being so down on myself all the time.

It was Halloween day, and though I was back at school and back in my routine, I tried not to be back in my old ways. I had a quiz in the class I had gotten an F in. I was ecstatic to find that I had earned a B this time. Working in study groups and trying to change the person that came on this campus was making a difference. That impact was definitely a good one.

I was starting to become a little more sociable with the

African-Americans on campus. When I had gotten back from homecoming, Blake, Shanay, Cammie, and I started hanging pretty tough. When we had cut through the surface of personalities, we realized that there weren't too many of us here, so we needed to stick together. I truly enjoyed Laurel. In fact, she was starting to become a part of me. Sometimes, though, you still need to be with your own people.

That day Cammie, Shanay, Blake, and I were all sitting in the cafeteria when we saw a group of girls sitting across from us. Everyone sitting with me refused to go talk to them because they thought they weren't freshmen. I didn't really think it made any difference.

"I remember when you guys just stared at me when y'all saw me in here. That was so uncomfortable. You guys can be rude if you want, but I'm going to go speak."

About two hours later, we all hooked up and went to the Athens mall. They were freshmen and were really cool. There was Erin, Andreta, Autumn, and Nica. I had told Autumn that I loved her name, and it later became known that it was because my middle name is Autumn.

On Halloween night, we had decided to go as cheerleaders to the football party. It would be perfect because we nearly had a whole squad.

"So do y'all know cheers?" I asked as we went to the pro shop and picked up some cheap uniforms.

"Girl," Shanay said, "this is just for show. You know, to show my legs."

"I know that's right," Blake seconded.

"I know; I just thought we could play the part."

"We will play the part. We will be cute, just like cheerleaders."

"Y'all are so crazy," I said.

I don't know how they did it, but somehow they talked me into coming out of my room. I thought the uniforms at

Lucy Laney were short, but this was just ridiculous.

"Girl, you look cute. Just come on," Shanay said. "When we get there, you need to hook me up with Dakari. It ain't like y'all are still talking."

I rolled my eyes at the thought. I thought she knew I wasn't completely through with this thing. I figured she'd get to the party, find an older football player, and forget all about Dakari.

"Fellas, look at the freshmen crew poppin' up in here! Daaang! Y'all look good," the fly guy working the door said to us.

Shanay and Blake walked by, and he hit them on their behinds. I was next in line, and he wasn't even gonna try me. I looked at him in a way to let him know.

"All right, sistah," he replied, reading the expression on my face. "I respect that, but you're gonna have to save me a dance. Maybe I can touch you then."

"Ohhh!" Cammie said as she pushed me through the door. "Girl, he was trying to get with you."

"Who is he?"

"He's the starting running back, Randall Hope."

"I hear he's about to lose his job. That new freshman is pulling it in," Autumn said.

Cammie turned and said, "That's Payton's old boyfriend."

"Who? The new freshman guy? Oh, he is so cute. Old boyfriend? Girl, what's wrong with you? I would've kept him."

I was so embarrassed. I wanted to go somewhere and hide. They were just too into my business.

"You know," I said to the girls later that night, "we don't have to stay together all night. Let's split up and have a good time."

About half an hour later, after I had danced with a few guys, I did a double take when I saw Dakari on the dance floor.

"Dang," I mumbled to myself.

As the crowd cleared, I saw he was really into his dance partner. As they turned while feeling the groove, my mouth dropped open when I saw Shanay with her hands around his waist.

Oh, gosh, I thought. *She's got him.*

She had it going on. She had pulled her skirt up a few inches and steam started streaming out of my ears when I noticed him rubbing her legs.

Quickly I dashed to the bathroom.

This just can't be happening, I said to myself. *I've got to get him back.*

No quicker had I opened the door, than a tear streamed down my face as soon as I laid eyes on Dakari and Shanay who were in the hallway kissing crazily. I don't even remember him kissing me like that.

I was angry at myself. Why couldn't I do that? Why couldn't I give him what he wanted when he wanted it? I'm sure if I tried to give it to him now he wouldn't want it anyway. It was always too late.

I wiped my eyes. I hated who I was. At that moment, I was becoming someone else.

10

Reaping
No Benefits

*L*ooking at them kissing, I just wished I was more secure. I wished I wasn't so wishy-washy. This back-and-forth feeling, this being between two guys, this feeling one way one minute and then feeling another way the next, was getting on my nerves.

As I tried to pick up my feet and walk past them, I couldn't move. I was just staring at them as if they were on the big screen or something. With their lips locked together and their heads moving from one side to the other, they were really into it. I was really watching. The tears kept falling, and I couldn't do anything about it.

Cammie saw and asked, "What's wrong?"

"I've got to get out of here," I told her. "I've got to go."

I went over to the drink table and chugged some punch. I knew it had alcohol in it, but at that moment I wanted that diversion. I didn't want to feel the pain. I knew in my heart that I shouldn't take a drink, but I did it anyway.

"I do all the work, and everybody else gets to reap the

benefits. This is crap!" I said as I threw the cup onto the floor.

"That's not the trash can," the cute running back that was sitting on the table said to me.

"Well, pick it up and put it in the trash can!" I exclaimed loudly.

"Oh, so you're going to front on me now. C'mon, where's my dance?" he said as he grabbed my hand and spun me around.

I said, "Whoo!" as I lifted up my skirt slightly.

I was angry, depressed, and upset, so my actions made no sense at all. I wanted to be free to enjoy what I could of the night. The fact that Dakari was cuddled up with another and probably about to get some was not settling to my soul.

I thought, *If he can do this, I might as well be busy, too. The stupid jerk!*

When Randall Hope pulled me to him, I threw my hands in the air and did not resist.

I started chanting, "Party in here!" out loud.

Before I knew it, a slow song came on, and Randall and I were wrapped in a tight embrace. Before I could even feel uncomfortable, there came Shanay and Dakari dancing only a few feet away. They were kissing again. How ridiculous!

"Daaang, freshman! You need to take that somewhere else!" a football player yelled out to Dakari.

"I see you got on the same li'l outfit as that girl. Are all freshmen like that?" Randall said as he tried to grab my bottom.

I pushed him hard in the chest one time. He fell back a couple feet. A little harder and he would have been on the floor.

"No!" I said, placing my hand in the air and yelling as I walked past Dakari and Shanay. "Everybody ain't easy!"

The alcohol made me uneasy, but I still knew what I was doing. I tripped into them, making their lips unlock. Maybe it was evil, but I did it.

"Payton!" Shanay said to me.

"What?" I said, putting my hands to the side as if asking if she wanted a piece of me.

"I'll be right back," Dakari said to Shanay.

"Where are you going, baby?"

"Baby? Baby? A couple of kisses, and he's your baby?" I said, clearly jealous.

Dakari grabbed me by the arm and pulled me outside. I tried to get out of his grasp. He was too strong.

"Get your hands off me!" I shouted to him. "Get back! Move!"

"You don't want me when I wanna be with you, but you are acting like a fool when you see me with someone else. Payton, what's up with you? You didn't call a brotha back. You didn't want me. Did you expect me to wait around? I care about you and all, but really . . . "

"What? I'm not all that? Is that what you're trying to say? You got a disease one time when you left me for somebody else. What do you think you're gonna get up here? Kissing her all crazy in an open party. Y'all look stupid."

"I don't look stupid. You heard the fellas. I got props."

"So, you think you got game, huh? You think you're a player, and all the fellas are impressed? That ain't nothin'. It ain't nothin' to catch a girl who wants to be caught. Get props when you catch the one that nobody can get."

"What? You, Payton? I've been there and could've had that. I told you no last year in my bedroom."

"Don't flatter yourself. I would have stopped on my own."

In disgust, Dakari uttered, "Whatever."

We didn't get to finish our conversation because Shanay came outside, grabbed Dakari by the hand, and said, "Excuse me, Payton. We have some unfinished business."

Dakari and Shanay turned, walked away, and drove off in Dakari's car while I just stood there crying. I couldn't believe this was happening. I said all that stuff to him, but I didn't mean most of it. I still wanted him, but this latest stunt he pulled was not one I wanted to follow. I knew it was over between us. That fact alone was reason enough for another drink.

Who did I see right next to the punch bowl as I stumbled back inside? None other than Randall Hope. He was ready to rap.

"Did you run from this?" he said, implying he was too much for me.

"Yeah," I said all too quickly.

"So, are we gonna finish our dance? Don't be afraid, baby. I can be gentle."

"I don't know," I said, taking a quick gulp from my cup as Cammie came over to me.

"Daaang! There's a li'l somethin', somethin' in there. You better take your time. You don't really look like the drinking kind," Randall said, looking amused.

"She's not," Cammie retorted, grabbing my arm as she tried to pull me away from him. "C'mon, Payton, I think it's time to go."

"Can't nobody tell Payton what to think and do," I sputtered, snatching my arm back. "Shoot, I'm grown. I done left my mom and dad back home in Augusta."

"C'mon, Payton. We need to go before things get out of hand," Cammie replied, still trying to persuade me.

Cammie thought she had my back, but she was really getting on my nerves. Telling me what to do was getting old. She needed to understand that I didn't want her help.

"Cammie, I'm not going anywhere. Don't make me go off on you up in here," I threatened, ready to make a scene.

"Payton, what's wrong with you?" she replied. "Come here."

She pulled me outside. She tugged me so hard that she forgot her jacket. She turned to go back inside.

"We're leaving as soon as I get my coat," she told me.

"Whatever!" I told her.

"So are you waiting on me or what?" Randall asked as he came outside and stood beside me.

"What's your name again?" I asked.

"Randall."

"No, don't be so stuck on yourself. I'm waiting on my friend."

"Who, your friend Tad?"

"No, I'm not waiting on Tad. How do you know about Tad?"

"I asked around. Got the scoop on you. You need to leave the young boys alone and get with a man."

"A man, huh? You better watch out so that those young boys don't take your spot on the football field. Ah, didn't know the word was out?"

"Well, since we're on the subject, you know he's starting soon. He must think he gonna be regular now, but he's not taking my job."

"Excuse me?" I said to him, not believing he could be so sure.

"I said he's not taking my job. That's why he's somewhere hugged up with the Bible, and I'm here hugged up with you. I'm gonna have both his positions."

I gave him a crazy look. Then Cammie came out. Since I was out of it, I asked her to drive.

As I rode home, I realized that I didn't have all that much to cheer about. That was quite ironic seeing how I had dressed up as a cheerleader.

I was leaning way back in my Jeep, desperately trying to get rid of a headache. The ten-minute ride had been anything but smooth. If I had my full faculties, I would have known it was from Cammie not knowing how to drive a stick. She was tearing up my clutch, and I didn't even realize it until she tried to parallel park near the dorm. When I heard a loud thump, my eyes sprang open.

"Oh, my gosh!" she said. "Payton, I hit that car. I'm so sorry."

"Get out of the car. Just get out of the car," I said, not wanting to believe my ears.

"I hope it's not that bad," Cammie confessed.

Inside I could only hope she was right. Hopefully, the noise I heard wasn't as awful an incident as it sounded. However, after addressing the damage and seeing the steam flare up from my engine, I realized that I was in deep, deep trouble.

The front part of my car was smashed. Even worse was the car that Cammie had hit in front of me. The back of the green Camry was badly dented. The paint was missing, and the left side of the bumper was hanging to the ground.

"Oh, my gosh!" I panicked. "My dad's insurance is going to go up. This is horrible. I can't have any more accidents. I've already had two bad accidents in the eleventh grade. I'm not even supposed to let anybody drive my car because I'm the only one insured. Give me the keys. I've got to move my car."

"But we've got to wait for the police."

"I cannot wait for the police. You don't understand. This is not a good thing. Just get in the car, Cammie!" I shouted.

My car would barely move.

"It sounds like it's going to blow up," she said.

"It'll be fine. I've just got to move it to the other side of the parking lot. I've got to get it away from this car."

"But what about this person's car?"

"They won't know who did it."

"Are you just going to hit the car and run?"

Without a care about the other person, whom I did not

144

know, I answered, "It'll be all right, but I won't be if this goes on my record."

"Payton, I can't let you do that. I'll take responsibility for it. I was the one driving."

"You can't take responsibility for it. My dad will be furious. You just don't understand. Do you have money to pay for this person's car? You don't even have a car."

"I just can't see driving away."

"It's not like we hit a person!" I screamed, attempting to make her see the light. "It's just a stupid car! Let's go, so I can lie down. My neck is hurting from that jerk."

"You can't say anything about this," I said to her as we entered the building. "I've got to figure out what to do. I've got to take my car somewhere. It's OK for now since it's night."

"I just don't feel right about this, Payton," Cammie replied timidly.

Ticked, I replied, "Well, you should have told me you didn't know how to drive a stick."

"Well, you weren't in any condition to drive. I obviously know something, or else we wouldn't have made it home."

"Well, you shouldn't have parallel parked. The stupid parking lot was only a few feet away!"

"But you said you didn't feel good, so I didn't want you to have to walk."

"Cammie, just don't say anything. Keep your mouth shut."

What am I gonna tell my dad? I thought as I lay in my bed. *I can't tell him the truth. I'm not gonna tell him. Someone else is going to have to look at my car.*

Not knowing what to do, I picked up my phone and dialed some digits. I was hoping that the person I wanted to talk to would answer. It was quite late, but with no one else to talk to I called despite the hour.

"Yeah," the groggy voice said.

"Tad?" I said softly. "I need your help."

145

"Payton?"

"Who else would have the nerve to call you this late?"

"I didn't think you would call me at all. I haven't heard from you in a while. What's up?"

"I just had a car accident."

Sounding a little clearer he asked, "Are you OK?"

"Yeah, my neck hurts a little, but my car is messed up. I need your help. It's pretty bad. I just need you to look at it. I know your uncle works on cars, and sometimes you mess around with them. I know you don't have a curfew tonight, so do you mind coming out to see?"

"Payton, it's after one. Can't this wait until the morning?"

"It won't take long. I just need you to take a look and tell me what's up."

"All right," he said, sighing reluctantly. "I'll be there in a second."

"OK, I'll be out front."

"I did something stupid tonight," I told him a little while later in person. "I had a couple of drinks."

"So you couldn't parallel park? You are one of the best drivers I know."

"I guess."

"Why would you drink?"

"It's a long story."

I knew I couldn't tell him that it was because I was jealous seeing Dakari kissing another girl. At that moment I thought he would care. But it seemed like Tad had gotten over me and moved on. Sure, he was there for me when I needed him, but he seemed distant. As if he wanted to finish the job and go back home, not like he wanted to pet my hand, hold me, or tell me that it was going to be OK. He made it seem as if it was the friend thing and that was the end of it.

He told me that he didn't think I should drive the car, that I should call my dad in the morning. With the car

146

smoking, it was definitely unsafe to drive.

"Another car was involved, wasn't it?" he asked me candidly.

I wondered how he could tell. I was just going to say I hit a pole or something.

"I see the paint right there. There is green paint on your car. Where's the car that you hit?"

If Tad figured it out in the dark, then surely the damage was going to be more obvious in the morning.

"Huh?" I asked.

"Where's the other car?" he asked. "Did you talk to the other person? Did you get any information? Were they OK?"

"Huh?" I said, scared.

"Why don't you wanna tell me? What happened?"

"I kind of left the scene."

The good-boy act was starting to really get on my nerves. He didn't have to be so dumb to understand that if I hit another car it was going to be major. Surely he knew that.

"The damage of the other car wasn't that bad. It was just a little fender-bender type of thing. It was no big deal, so I left. Don't make it seem as if I'm this horrible person."

"Well, it seems like you've got your mind made up. I'm just a little disappointed in you," he scolded. "To think of yourself so selfishly and not even think about the consequences you're putting on somebody else just doesn't seem like the Payton I know. How do you expect good to come from that?"

Those were scary words. Hearing that only bad could come from my actions, I just didn't want to believe it. Especially when I had done everything I could to avoid conflict. My parents could never get mad at me and take my car away for hitting someone else. They would be severely mad because I had let someone else drive my car against their wishes.

No matter what Tad, Cammie, or anybody else thought, this was what I was going to do. It may not have been the nice or proper thing, but it was definitely the smart thing. I had to keep this under wraps, and that was all there was to it.

"Dad," I whined into the telephone the next morning.

"What's wrong, baby girl?"

"Daddy . . ."

I was trying to lay on the crybaby act so that he would feel sorry for me. When I told him what was wrong, he would know I was going through it and wouldn't feel the need to make me any more upset. It used to work in high school, so I figured I'd try it now.

"Girl, cut all that mess out. You're in college. Tell me what's going on. It's time to be a young woman and take responsibility for your actions. I can't help if you don't talk to me."

"My car, Dad. It's messed up."

"Payton Skky, that's pretty vague. What happened? You're not hurt or anything, are you?"

I told the biggest fib I had told in a while. I told him that no one was in the car but me when I hit a pole, my car was severely destroyed, and I was the only one driving.

I was so into this lie that I didn't even realize that of course I'd have to be driving if I was the only one in the car. I had just emphasized that I was the one driving, and that got my dad a little suspicious. Only, I didn't know it then.

He hung up the phone nicely. He told me not to worry about anything, that he could bring me a new car. He said he was just happy that I was OK.

Yeah, I knew that was what I was supposed to do, I thought. *Listening to Tad is going to get me in trouble.*

"That's awful," Laurel said as she was walking into the room.

"What? What's awful?" I asked, being nosy.

"You know Judy, our dorm director? Well, somebody hit her car last night and pulled off. She only had liability insurance, so she can't get it fixed. Isn't that terrible?" Laurel said to me.

"Well, what kind of car does she have?"

"A Toyota. It's old, but her whole fender is off. I just can't believe somebody would be that cruel to just leave, only thinking about themselves. That's awful. That's why more folks need to be Christians, because Christians wouldn't do stuff like this."

I felt so convicted at that moment that chills of anxiety went up my spine.

"Payton? Why aren't you saying anything? Isn't that terrible?" she asked me once again.

I heard the girl, but what could I say? *It was me! I'm the one who drove off and left the poor lady with no compensation for fixing her car! I'm the Christian who at this moment isn't actin' like one!* I don't think so. I didn't know what to say.

"I've got to go to the bathroom," I said quickly.

I really hated that when my suite mates were in the bathroom they never locked the door. I would sometimes just walk in and, though it seemed rude, it wasn't my fault because they didn't lock the door.

Anna was back. I didn't know if she was going to return after the incident, but she did. She was brushing her teeth. I wanted to walk right back out because for some reason, I had been avoiding her.

She grabbed my arm as I was about to walk away and put up one finger as if to say hold on. After cleaning herself up, she reached out to hug me.

"I've been trying to catch up with you, but you are such a busy person. My parents wanted to say thank you. Have you gotten my messages? I got you a card."

I nodded.

"Payton, I'm sorry for bugging you, but I just wanted to tell you that you are such a special person. If it weren't for you, I probably wouldn't be here. God used you to save my life, and I wanna know more about the God that you and Laurel talk about. I know He spared my life for a reason. You are such a good person. You don't do things that are bad or wrong. I know it's because you answer to a higher power, and I want to be like that."

OK, Lord, what are You trying to tell me? I thought. *I obviously made the wrong decision by hitting that car and walking away. I had a little bit to drink, but even with a clear mind I still wanted to act like it didn't happen, but it did happen. I'm responsible. I can't blame Cammie because she didn't know how to drive a stick. It was truly my fault. Forgive me, Lord. This is going to be hard to reverse.*

"Anna, I would love to talk to you about Christ, but I don't know everything. In fact, I'm still growing myself. I know He is a forgiving God, and I'm definitely not perfect, even though the Lord's Spirit is in me. I don't always let the Spirit dominate. Sometimes Payton leads. Do you know what I'm sayin'?"

"Yeah," she answered genuinely. "You're saying that you're real."

"So now when I wanna let Payton lead, the Lord taps me on the shoulder with a little reminder that my choices aren't the best ones. I don't wanna get into it, but this is one instance He used you to help me see that."

"Really?"

"Yeah. I apologize that I haven't really been around. I don't know what my deal was. It's just been really weird. The whole incident was hard."

"It was hard for me too. Looking at that tub and knowing that it could have been the last place I was. Thankfully, that wasn't the case."

"Yeah."

"We got off on the wrong foot, too, Payton. I was following Jewels's vibes with the whole black thing."

"Anna, don't worry about it—"

"No, let me say this," she cut in. "I didn't even know you, and I judged you because of the color of your skin. Nothing good comes from all of that. If it wasn't for that black chick who stayed home on Friday night, who knows what would have become of me? You're a beautiful girl, Payton. I'm sorry that I didn't see you for who you were in the beginning. I'm glad you're my suite mate. I'm so glad you were there for me, even though you could've just walked away."

"Like I would really leave you in here."

We hugged.

"Anna," I said quickly, "I need to confess some stuff, too."

"What?"

"You've gotta sit down for this one."

After telling her, she said, "Oh, Payton. Are you serious? Was that you?"

"I wanna make it right, and I'm going to. I just don't know how. I'll tell Judy it was me, but I won't have a car for a while. I don't believe this."

"What?" Anna asked. "What don't you believe?"

"I can't believe my response to it all."

"I actually understand."

I knew it wasn't going to be easy telling Judy that I was the one responsible for the damage to her car. Tad, Cammie, Anna, and Laurel were right. Nothing good was going to come from me continuing to cover up for my mistakes. I had to face them, learn from them, and grow to be more like Christ because of them. I had to let Jesus work out all the rest of it. I wasn't perfect, and I couldn't pretend that I was. It says in the Word, "You reap what you sow." I hadn't done

151

anything good at that point, and so I was reaping no benefits.

11

Planting Hopeful Seeds

"Am I supposed to just forgive you and not want to press charges?" Judy, the dorm director, said to me.

"Well, she really is sorry," Laurel explained when she saw I couldn't move my mouth.

That was a good question Judy asked. I took the low road, which was the road to nowhere. Now I wanted to skate through the consequences and act like nothing bad had happened.

Overcome with emotion, I sat on her bed and sobbed. "You're right, Judy. I know I caused a lot of damage, which I'll pay for. I know it was wrong, and I'm sorry. My dad is on his way up here, so if you want to go down to the police station and file a full report, go ahead. I'll be here, but I just want you to know that I am truly sorry. Will you please forgive me for hitting your car and trying to get out of the consequences?"

I started to walk out of the door, trying to gain my composure, but Judy stopped me. "I guess I appreciate that apology more than hearing you say, 'I'm the one who wrecked your car, and I'll pay for it,' " she said, sarcastically mocking me. "And yes . . . I will forgive you."

I didn't say that at first. I don't know what I was thinking. When you do something so ruthless, sometimes you have to be extremely apologetic to be forgiven. I was thankful that in the end she saw that I was truly sorry.

Laurel didn't walk me back to the room. Instead, she went on to gymnastics. I wished she would have stayed around so that she could ease the tension that would occur when my dad arrived. I didn't know how I was going to tell him the truth. However, she couldn't, so I had to stand on my own. I was still grateful for the hug that she gave me and for sticking up for me.

"It'll be OK," Laurel told me. "Just pray and tell the truth."

"You don't know my dad," I expressed with tears in my eyes.

"Well, God knows him. He can't get too mad."

"OK, you go on. I don't want you to be late for practice."

As I lay on my bed, depressed and waiting for my doom, the phone rang. Looking at the clock, I was sure it was my dad saying that he was not too far away. However, when I picked it up, I was very surprised to find it was Dakari. I wasn't sure if that was a good or bad thing considering he was lip-locked with another the night before.

"Are you OK?"

"Yeah," I said, trying to be nonchalant.

"Your boy told me you were in an accident."

I wanted so desperately to say, "Why do you care? It's all your fault. Cammie wouldn't have been driving if I hadn't been drunk. I wouldn't have been drunk if you had not been all up on Shanay."

However, I knew that ultimately I was responsible for my actions. No one forced me to take a sip. Though Dakari was in it, he wasn't to blame.

"You know you don't drink, and you shouldn't have had anything," he said, scolding me.

"Don't even go there," I lashed out in anger. "When did you find out? This morning when you came in from being out all night with Shanay?"

"I knew you would act like this. Didn't nothin' happen."

"Oh, really? Is that supposed to make me feel better? Don't say nothin' happened, because I saw y'all kissing at the party. Then you left with her, so I'm sure you took the kissing with you."

"So you care?"

"No!" I yelled back as loud as my lungs could scream.

"Then why do you have my every move mapped out like you had been watching me all night?"

"You cared that I got into a car accident."

"Yeah, I told you that's why I was calling. Look, just because you decided not to kick it with me doesn't mean that I still don't have thoughts of you."

"Oh, you have thoughts of me the day after an all-nighter with another girl."

"I don't want to get into a fight with you. I just wanted to call and see if you were OK. I thought we could bury the hatchet. Though I was with Shanay, you were the only one on my mind. Maybe we could give this thing another try, but I ain't calling for all that. I just wanted to make sure you were OK. All right?"

"Yeah, all right," I said after much hesitation.

"Daddy, why are you taking my car away?" I cried.

"Payton, you can't even drive this car. You told me you didn't hit anybody. That was a lie. You broke down and told me you weren't the one driving. Now, that is a nightmare. What if the other girl in the car would've gotten hurt? Or, what if there was someone in the other car? I'm not giving you another car after all. You need to learn to be more responsible. If you don't have a car, I think you will appreciate it more when or if you get one back."

That sounded crazy to me, but he was the father. Reluctantly, I had to oblige. This was horrible news. Walking?

"Don't look so down, baby girl. Maybe I spoke too soon. This isn't forever. I'll probably give you your car back when you come home for Christmas."

"How am I supposed to get home?" I spoke with an attitude, even though I knew I should have been respectful.

"The bus sounds like a good idea to me, and if you keep getting smart with me you will still be riding the bus after Christmas."

"Sorry, Dad."

Dad took Laurel and me out for dinner that night when she returned from gymnastics. I guess he felt a little guilty about not leaving me with a car, and I guess he thought that this was a way to make up for it. Laurel just kept talking through dinner. It was cool with my father because he liked getting to know her. He even said he thought Laurel was great.

"Payton and I keep each other in line," she told my daddy.

"Oh, so you need some straightening out, too, huh?" my father said, joking.

"Oh, no, I always tell the truth. I don't do anything bad like Payton," she said, joking back.

I kicked Laurel in the shin from under the table. Laurel was great, but sometimes she put her foot in her mouth when she didn't think before she spoke. That comment must have made me look horrible in the eyes of my dad, even though it was a joke.

"Yeah, I know Miss Payton is a handful. So what's up with the young men here at UGA?"

Laurel almost spit out her food. I had never told her that my dad and I were really tight. I could talk to him. I had only pulled apart from him last year when I thought I knew everything. If I had only listened to some of the advice he had previously given me, maybe I wouldn't have the drama I have now.

"Dad, she likes her old boyfriend from high school. He goes to Georgia. The only problem is he likes someone else."

"That sounds like your situation, Payton."

"Almost," I teased back. "Only difference is that I have two old boyfriends here."

My dad got serious and replied, "Well, you guys need to stay focused on your studies. Don't focus on these boys. Get yourself together, and then all the boys will come to you."

That took me back to last year when my principal, Dr. Franklin, told me the very same thing. In retrospect, it worked. When I had gotten over Dakari and moved on to Tad, Dakari came crawling back.

My dad continued, "You young ladies should be the dream catch for any man worth having. Beauty, brains, standards . . . you should be a gift to any guy. Choose one that will take care of the present you are. You all may come up against quite a few knuckleheads up here on campus, but believe me, there is a man made just for you. Payton, I know your mom was just for me, and I did everything I could to catch her. With all the fast girls running behind me, your mom refused to chase me or any other man. I knew with her, I had to come correct. She was on many guys' list. That was because she wasn't lying down with no man she wasn't married to. All my friends wanted to be the guy that got her in the end. She was a confident brown fox, and I just had to have her. As the story went, I won her heart. Girls, don't settle for nothing less than what you know in your heart is the very best in a man. You both deserve that."

Dad had a good point. I needed to work on me and get myself in order. I was going to take Dad's advice. I hugged him tightly at the dinner table.

"Oh, so you're gonna listen now?"

"Yeah, I'm gonna have a lot of extra time to spend in my dorm now that I don't have a car. I can think about what you said and figure out how to apply it to my life. I just love your wisdom, Dad."

"Don't try to suck up to me, Payton. I'm not going to change my mind."

"You guys have a neat relationship," Laurel said as she watched us. "I miss my father. I'll have to call him."

"I'm sure your dad would enjoy that very much. I know it makes my day when Payton calls me and she doesn't want anything."

We all laughed.

"Baby, what do you want for Christmas . . . besides a car?" my dad asked.

With a pure heart I said, "I'd love some of your self-confidence wrapped neatly in a box, with a pretty bow on top."

He responded, "You have that."

"Not like you, Daddy. I wish. No, seriously, I don't need anything for Christmas. I know that I'm already blessed."

"So," he kept prying, "you don't want anything?"

"Well, you can always hook your first good bullet up with some clothes," I teased.

He smiled. "I thought there was something."

"I just wanted to let you know I was OK," I said to Tad three days after the accident.

"Dakari told me he talked to you, and you sounded fine."

"Your discussion seems kind of short."

"Yeah, I've got some studying because I just came in from practice. We've got a big game this week. I'm just trying to stay focused."

"Am I distracting you?" I asked softly.

"Frankly, yes. I'm glad you called to let me know you are OK, but I really need to get back to work."

Even though he was nice about hurting my feelings, it still hurt. But I understood. Just like Dakari wanted fifty thousand chances with me, I was doing the same thing to Tad. His tolerance was short, and though I had a tough time swallowing that, I had to respect it.

"I didn't really talk that long with Dakari, but I did want to let you know that I thought about what you said, and I took back what I did."

Confused, Tad spoke out, "What? You took back what you did? What are you talking about?"

"I asked Judy, my dorm director, to forgive me, and told her I would pay for the damages. I appreciate you telling me the tough stuff."

"Well, we fall, but we get back up," he told me.

"What do you mean?"

"Sometimes sinners sin—it's this song I'm listening to by Donnie McClurkin."

"Well, that's easy for you to say. You don't make any mistakes."

"You've only known me for a year. You weren't there the night Jesus found me. You don't know how miserable my life was. God saved me from a horrible place. Even my thoughts of you drive me crazy. One day you like me, and then the next you like someone else. I get quite angry when you flip-flop like that. Why do you get all worked up over a guy who likes you one day and then the next he likes five other girls? You deserve better."

Tad was right. I did deserve better. I thought about what my dad had said to Laurel and me at dinner. Dakari always knew how to reel me in, though. I was the only one who could stop that, and it was about time that I did.

"I never understood why girls fall for a jerk and then when that doesn't work out, they run to the good guy to pick up the pieces. I'm tired of being with folks who don't respect me. If a woman doesn't respect me now, she'll never be able to respect me in a marriage. That's what God calls a wife to do, respect her husband."

There was dead silence on the line. So much so that you could hear a pin drop on a carpeted floor. I didn't know what to say. I didn't like Dakari any more than I liked Tad. Even though it was obvious that Tad was a way better boyfriend than Dakari, I could only see that they were equal. No wonder Mr. Taylor was frustrated. Maybe hearing him say it would make me appreciate that good guy a little more.

Dear Lord, I prayed later that week, *help me get my act together. Help me be the kind of lady that You want me to be. Help me learn to study Your word. Help me have the desire above all things to please You and make You proud. I used to think I was so much better than Rain, Lynzi, and Dymond when it comes to pleasing You, but I'm not. I may even be worse. Help me get up and stand strong. Help me be a child after Your own heart. I love You. Amen.*

I had been doing so much better in my classes. By asking questions and studying, I was definitely confident that a flag would never appear on my paper again. I had talked for so long about wanting to feel better about myself. Some days were good days, and some days were bad. So many things dictated the way that I felt.

A Scripture my Papa Skky used to say was, "God has not given us a spirit of fear, but of power and of love and of a sound mind." I always used to tell him, "I can't do it, Papa; I'm scared." He would then always repeat the Scripture. When I got older, he explained what the Scripture meant.

What was I scared of? I was afraid of coming to college and failing and letting everybody down. I was intensely scared of not being loved by a guy whom I thought I liked or loved. Yet, when it boiled down to it, the only thing that matters is that I am happy with myself, and love what God created. Now this didn't mean accepting and liking the bad things that were inside of me—God calls those things sin. What it did mean was trusting God for who He made me to be. God doesn't make mistakes. He made me just the way I am for a purpose, and I wanted to accomplish the purpose He has for me.

I was tired of being down, afraid, and miserable. I was going to change that, and changing it didn't mean doing so for a little while. It meant forever.

After racking my brain figuring out how I was going to maintain my self-esteem, accept the way I was, and honor God with the life He had given me, God led me to one of my birthday gifts. It was the book from Tad, *A Jewel in His Crown*.

Just by reading the introduction, I was encouraged. The book was about all the things that I had issues believing. Tad gave me the book because he thought I was a special, precious gem. After reading, I began to understand we are all made in God's image. Nothing else in all of God's creation was made in His image except man. The God of the universe made us so that He could have a relationship with us. That's so sweet! I was now beginning to understand why God loves us so much. Through that love, I could love others and, most important, love God back.

I had a paper to write, but I vowed to pick up the book again very soon.

"So are you mad at me?" Cammie asked at lunch.

"No, why would you ask that?"

"Laurel told me that your dad took your car away."

"Girl, sit down. I wanted to be angry at everybody except myself. I owe you for being there. Had you not been there, there's no telling what would have happened. Shoot, I could be dead."

"I still owe you an apology," she said humbly. "I should have told you that I didn't know how to drive a stick."

"You can drive; you just need some practice. I owe you an apology for not being the friend I should have been when it all went down. I was just freaked out and responded the wrong way."

"I appreciate that. I don't have many friends. It's not easy for me to make them. I'm not spunky or petite like you. You have two fine guys after you."

"Well, that doesn't make me who I am. Acceptance from others doesn't make you who you are. Shanay, who is supposed to be my friend, was the reason why I was so upset at the party. She and Dakari left together."

"Did they get their freak on?"

"You so crazy. Dakari says they didn't, but I don't trust him. I'm sure the other girls saw me upset, but you were the only one who came to my aid. That tells a lot about you. You could've gone and had a good time, but instead you made sure I got home safely. Cute people are great to walk around with, but they aren't worth anything if they don't care about you. You are cute, and you are a great friend."

"Thanks, Payton."

"I believe God wants us to trust Him. I challenge you to believe that. I'm reading this book that talks about being a diamond in God's eyes. Diamonds are rare, and so are we. We've just got to believe it."

She reached over and hugged me. Neither of us was like a rooted, grounded tree, strong and sturdy. However, I was thankful that in the area of trusting God for who we were, we were planting hopeful seeds.

12

Seeing the Blessings

$\mathscr{A}$s I walked around the campus late on Sunday afternoon, I pondered the message the pastor had preached earlier that day.

"Keep Sowing . . . Your Harvest Is on the Way" was the topic. He had gotten it from Matthew 13:3–8. It basically talked about a man who sowed four times before there was a benefit. The first three times the sower tried to produce a crop, something happened that didn't allow a harvest.

As I thought about my own life and the things that I wanted this semester in college, I got a little discouraged because it hadn't worked out like I planned. The message let me know that I just had to keep on trying, keep on praying, and keep on working hard, so that I could reap. Though I couldn't see the end result, God's words let me know that I had to keep trying, and eventually I would produce the things that I desired.

However, the problem was that most of the things that I wanted were not spiritual things. I just recently understood that, in order to accept myself, I needed to trust God for who He made me to be and know my worth in Christ. How can I really fully comprehend that if I'm not doing the things that Christ calls me to do?

There could be frustration because every time I tried to pick up that book that Tad had given me, something came up that I really needed to do. I made a commitment to make sure to study the Word, and I had fallen short in that goal. However, going back to the message of the day, I realized that I could start again. I'd just keep starting over until I developed the kind of relationship with Christ that He's proud of, and one that I'm happy about.

"Hey, Payton! Wait up. What are you doing out here so late? It'll be getting dark soon. I thought females weren't supposed to walk alone on campus."

"I keep forgetting about the time change. How are you doing, Mr. SGA man?"

"Oh, so now you got jokes," Karlton said to me.

"How have you been?"

"I've been good. Are you going to join my committee or what? I'm tryin' to get you involved."

"Well, my experience here this semester has not been the best. I don't think I could convince other people to come here," I said, being honest.

"Well, I think that's because you and honest people would really appreciate getting serious and truthful answers. Therefore, they may commit to UGA. Why don't you come to my committee meeting next week, and if you like what we are doing, you can join. If you don't, I won't bother you anymore. Is that cool?"

"Yeah! How have you been?"

"I've thought about you, and, as I can see, you still look good."

"Thank you," I said.

"Has your semester been rough?" he asked.

"Yeah, like I said, I don't think I could convince anyone to come here, but I'm surviving, and I like that. It's showing me some qualities that I didn't even know I had. I'm doing OK."

"Well, I guess that explains why you haven't given a brotha a call."

"Yeah," I quickly answered.

"You got it goin' on, Payton Skky. I don't wanna push you, but I do wanna get to know you. I think I can make this transition a little easier for you."

I appreciated what he was saying. He was older. He was involved in activities, and he wanted to help me out. He was definitely a good person. However, I wanted to do it on my own. If I had any assistance from anybody, it would be from God. I was so proud that I was thinking that way. I didn't say anything to Karlton because I didn't want to be rude. I just simply thanked him, gave him an innocent hug, and walked inside to study.

"Well, Miss Skky," my English teacher said to me, "what a difference in your work."

I was so excited when I saw a B staring back at me from the top of the page. I had read Hamlet from front to back. I knew quite a bit of the story, and Laurel had read it in high school, so the parts that I didn't really understand she gave me some assistance with. Two weeks ago when we were assigned this story, my grade wasn't so favorable. Fortunately, I learned that when you study hard, results happen.

My mouth hung open when she announced the next book. It was *The Color Purple*. Not only had I seen the movie a hundred times, but I had also read the book. It was a really good story of a woman struggling and trying to break free—not just from her husband but from fear of failure in herself.

This was going to be interesting.

"We're gonna have to come to your dorm if we have any questions," one of the girls in my class said to me.

In my mind I said, *They never offered for me to come and study books that are similar to them.* But then again, I never asked.

I just said, "Sure, I'm very familiar with this story. Call me." I handed her a piece of paper with my phone number on it.

Before I walked out of the class, the teacher stopped me and explained why she had chosen *The Color Purple.* She learned from one of her own professors that the best lit teachers included writings from as many cultures as possible. She hoped I wasn't uncomfortable. I thought that was weird considering it was a book from my heritage. However, some parts of the book I couldn't relate to, because back in those days blacks weren't allowed to go to UGA. I thanked God we had come this far, but we still had so much farther to go. With that thought, I decided to take Karlton up on his offer and become a member of his minority recruitment committee.

"No, ma'am," I said to the teacher, getting back to her question. "I'm excited about reading *The Color Purple.* I think it's a great read and a deep story. I'm not offended at all. See ya."

"Keep up the good work," she said as I walked out of the door.

I was busy trying to study when I heard someone banging on the door. Laurel was at gymnastics, and I had no idea where my suite mates were. Maybe Jewels had locked herself out. However, if that was the case then she was rude for pounding on the door.

"Dang! I'm coming!" I screamed.

When I opened it, I wanted to slam it when I saw Shanay standing before me. She was with Blake. They scurried their way into my room without an invitation.

"What do I owe the pleasure? Oops, I don't know if it's a pleasure. Why are y'all here?" I said sarcastically.

Shanay just kept smiling at me, and I had no idea why.

"Don't sit on my bed," I said as I noticed she was about to plop down.

What in the world did they want? I wasn't really mad at Blake because I heard she was talking to some sophomore. This meant that she'd left Tad alone, at least for the time being. However, they were both sneaky, and I didn't like that one bit. They weren't the kind of friends I wanted.

"What do you guys want?" I repeated after becoming tired of looking at their fake smiles. "I've got studying to do."

"It sounds like you're trying to get rid of us," Shanay said.

"Oh, so you caught that," I joked, trying to be funny.

"Look," Shanay explained, "I just came because I don't wanna lose your friendship over a guy."

"What do you mean? I saw you at the party all over Dakari."

"I know, but I pulled back in the end."

"He told me he stopped it."

"Whatever, him . . . me . . . point is we stopped. He is still hung up on you, and I don't have time for that. He's cute and all, but I just don't have time to waste."

"I told you we still had feelings for each other."

"Yeah, but you also told Blake that you liked some other football player. How was I supposed to know? Then we heard that you were dating some guy in SGA."

"Karlton? No, we just went out once," I defended.

"See," Shanay cut in, "y'all are dating. You can't blame me for thinking it was over with you and Dakari. Don't worry about that, because there is this starting running back, Randall Hope. After I left Dakari, I headed back over to the party, and things got interesting."

She was crazy. One minute she was ready to give it up to one guy, and the next she was ready to give it up to another. She was completely gone. How was anyone supposed to respect her when she obviously didn't respect herself? She acted as if she was proud of her actions. Though I was torn between two guys, I wasn't ready to give it up to either of them.

"So, Blake, what do you think?" I asked.

Blake replied, "Well, Shanay and I think somewhat different."

"Y'all are just like me. You just don't want to admit it," Shanay said.

I attacked, "Tuh! That couldn't be further from the truth."

"Well, that's why you've got Dakari all frustrated," Shanay said. "You act as if you wanna give it up, and then the next minute you wanna take it back. That is so tacky."

"At least it's a lot more admirable than being out there," I told her candidly.

"Are you trying to call me a . . . ?"

I cut her off by saying, "Look, I'm not trying to call you anything. It's your life; do your own thing."

"Don't worry, I did, and I will keep on doing it," Shanay responded rudely.

"Don't get no attitude up in my room. You can always get out."

"We didn't come here for all of that," Blake said, trying to ease the tension. "I came to apologize. Some of the girls told me you were really upset and drank some of that punch. I don't really remember much else, but I guess I should have been there for you."

Without her saying much else, I realized that she had been intoxicated, too.

"The next day I promised myself that I would never drink like that again. I had no reason to do so," Blake confessed.

I then realized that I had no reason to drink either. Regardless of what Dakari and Shanay did, it should have never driven me to drink. When I had problems, I needed to get down on my knees and not turn to liquor.

"Anyway, I wondered why you hadn't returned my calls," she asked.

"You called me?" I asked in return.

Blake replied, "Yeah."

So much was going on. Maybe she had called, and I had dismissed it in anger. I couldn't remember.

"I just came to ask you for forgiveness," Blake said genuinely.

"Yeah, girl," Shanay added. "I like Dakari, but I noticed that there were too many fine brothas to be tied down to him. So what's up? Are we cool?"

I was so happy that they understood my viewpoint, and that I had misread Blake's actions. By them coming over to my dorm, I realized that college friendships were gonna be hard to have and maintain. However, I didn't want to be alone, and I wasn't perfect. Who knows? In the future I might let them down. I was somewhat blessed to have them, and I went over and gave them both big hugs.

I wasn't being fake. I did mean it. However, I was going to keep an eye out for Shanay—and Blake too.

"Y'all can sit on my bed," I joked.

I was never big on soul food. Seafood was my passion. However, being away and eating campus meals, I was craving some collard greens. Thanksgiving couldn't come too soon for me.

"What a joy it is to have you helping me this morning, Miss Payton," my mom said as I was cutting the onions.

My dad's two sisters and my grandparents were visiting. Dinner was going to be at twelve. My uncle Percy and his family were coming for Christmas. I actually missed Pillar. But I'd have to wait a month to see her.

I had gotten in so late on Wednesday night that I hadn't had the chance to call my friends. I was only going to be home for a couple of days, so I wanted to maximize my time with my family and friends.

"What, Payton?" my mom asked as she noticed I had stopped cutting the onions.

"You're just so beautiful," I said to her. "I hope that when I get into my late forties I will be as beautiful."

"Well, that is a sweet thing to say. I think I like you being away at college," she said, laughing.

"You don't miss me, huh?" I candidly asked.

I don't know if it was the onions or if I was really emotional, but the tears were sprinkling down my face.

"Payton," my mother called out with seriousness, "how dare you say such a thing? Of course I miss you. I was just kidding. I remember when you were just a little baby in my arms, and now you are all grown up. I remember sitting on your bed, wondering why you couldn't be here with me instead of off in college. I was blessed because you were still somewhere. Though I am your mother, you truly belong to God. I am in no position to clip your wings or be angry at God for letting you move on. You are such a blessing. Is that your phone?" my mom said to me as she cut off her thoughts.

I dashed to my room, sure it had to be one of my girls. It had to be Rain, Dymond, or Lynzi. I was surprised to hear Dakari's voice.

"What are you doing calling me this early? Don't you sleep in?"

"Yeah, I was going to stay at the dorm, but I decided to

come home. I'm going back in the morning. My brother plays the Detroit Lions today."

"Oh, really?"

"Yeah, I'm having a get-together with the crew. Call your girls and see if they wanna come."

"I'm not gonna set up your party for you. I haven't even talked to them yet. What time is the game?"

"At four."

"Well, if I talk to them we might stop by."

"What else are you gonna be doing? You know you'll get tired of hanging with the family."

"Actually I miss them, Dakari!"

"We haven't talked in a while, so do you miss me? I know you do," he said in a sexy voice.

"You're trippin'. I might see you later, but I might not. Either way, happy Thanksgiving."

I hung up and smiled. I was becoming a bigger person. I could focus on this friendship. My heart no longer raced when I heard his voice. Dakari Graham and Payton Skky could be friends.

I looked out of the window and said, "Thanks, Lord. Thank You for helping me."

Perry crept into my room and said, "Mom said she thought you were supposed to be helping her, not talking on the phone."

"What are you doing to help? I don't see nothin' wrong with your hands."

"I'm not a girl."

"And? You want to eat, don't you?"

I took my pillow and threw it at his head. Neither of us meant any of it. We were just happy to see each other.

"All right, I'll help," he said.

I grabbed him around the neck and said, "Mom, put us to work."

Most of the food was prepared. My mom loved this kind

of stuff. However, it was time to set the table, and that was where Perry and I stepped in. I thought about Tad. I had no idea how he was doing. I could only pray that he was doing well and that he was happy.

"Are you and Tad dating or what?" my nosy brother asked, placing the fork on the wrong side of the plate.

"It doesn't go there, Perry. The forks go on the left side," I said, getting frustrated.

"Y'all must not be because you are a little tight with that question. What did you do to turn him away? He was a good guy."

"What about you and your girlfriend? How are y'all doing?"

"I don't know. She's still my girl, but it's hard trying to keep my eyes focused on one girl."

"Well, if that's the case, you need to tell her," I told him, sensing that his life was about to get interesting.

I was glad we had a good relationship. I loved Perry, and he loved me back. That was such a blessing.

Later that Thanksgiving afternoon, my family sat around the extralong table that was adorned in my mom's china and crystal. Before we ate, my grandfather led us in prayer.

He humbly spoke, "Dear heavenly Father, we come this day to give thanks for so much You have done for us. We also thank You for sending Your Son to die for our sins. Lord, You don't have to be so good to us, but You are, and at this very moment, we are seeing the blessings."

13

Passing Whichever Test

"here are you going?" my mother asked as I grabbed my dad's keys and started to head out of the door that Thanksgiving Day.

I was in college, but I was still her child. I didn't want her to worry about my whereabouts. I knew I was going over to Dakari's house, and I didn't want her to misread anything. This was strictly a friendship thing.

"There's gonna be a whole group of us going over to Dakari's to watch his brother's game. It just gives me a chance to get together with my friends. Dymond is leaving the day after tomorrow."

"Payton, your aunts are here all the way from New York and Dallas."

"But we already ate, and I talked to them. If you want me to stay I will," I told her, practically biting my tongue.

"Just be respectful. I hope you aren't lying to me, and there really is going to be a big group over there."

I wanted to be mad that my mother would suspect such

a thing, but how could I be when she had caught me in that type of stuff before?

However, I was now a new me and whatever I told her gave her confidence. I had already told her pretty much what she needed to know regarding Dakari and myself. She just had to trust me. The earlier comment about her being pretty helped. She finally agreed I could go.

As I got into my father's car and turned the key, I realized that I didn't tell her that Dakari's parents weren't going to be home. Since she didn't ask, I didn't tell.

"What are you thinking about so heavily?" Rain asked as she jumped into the car.

"Girl, you scared me."

"I know. I was waving to you while I was walking out here. Something heavy must be on your mind. What's going on?"

"Nothing; I'm just trying to check myself. Give me a hug, girl."

I couldn't begin to explain in the embrace how much I missed her. But as tight as it was, I was sure she got the point.

"What is Dakari having and why do you insist that I go?"

"Girl, you're trippin'. I didn't insist that you go. You're the one who is complaining because Tyson didn't come home, and you don't have any plans. How are y'all doing?"

"Hangin' on," she said in a sad tone. "I think we're just going through a rough period. One time Tyson came to pick me up, and I saw his eyes wandering."

"What?"

"Yes, he acts as if he has never seen beautiful black women. We're together, and I still love him, but we're holding on by a very thin thread."

"Well, you act like it's cool. Is it cool with you?"

"For a minute I thought I wasn't pretty, because it seemed as if he was looking at everyone but me. However, he has got things going on, and I am giving him the benefit of the doubt."

"Even if he doesn't tell you, you should feel good about yourself."

"Yeah, but Spelman is a totally different world. Most girls go to class all dressed up to impress one another. Can you believe that! I don't think my freshman class has learned to be content with who they are yet. I hope you aren't going to Dakari's because you guys are back together. Tell me that is not the case, and where is Tad?"

"You sound like my brother. Don't even go there."

"Oooh, girl. Don't hold out on me. What's up?"

"I don't know. We are all just going in different directions. It's good to see you," I said as I patted her on the arm.

"You better keep your hand on the steering wheel. From what I hear, you aren't having too much luck with cars lately."

"Girl, I've been driving since I was eleven."

We raced up to Dymond's door. Her mom was glad to see us. She was still the same ghetto, sweet woman she had always been.

"Y'all think y'all are big-time now, don't y'all?" she said to us. "Goin' to Spelman, Howard, and UGA. Can't tell y'all nothing now! You look like you put on a few pounds, Payton. You look good, girl."

I pulled Dymond and Rain into the car and asked, "Do I look fat to y'all?"

"You don't need anyone's approval," Rain said to me sarcastically, repeating what I had said to her earlier.

While in the car, I noticed that Dymond was unusually quiet. She wasn't going on and on about her new world like she would have normally done. Instead, Rain, who was the quiet one, was going on and on. We were changing, but was that a good thing? Nonetheless, driving on our old streets with old friends was definitely a good thing.

"Why are we stopping at the store?" Dymond asked irritably. "If he is going to invite us over, then he needs to provide the food. This isn't a potluck, and don't expect me to buy anything."

College had definitely made Dymond a little different. She wasn't as giving. Why was that?

"What's your problem? You go up north for a minute, and you come back mean," I told her.

"I'm not mean. I'm just straight up."

"Yeah," Rain put in, "you aren't giving any love, no hugs, no I miss yous, or anything. What's up?"

"Girl, after the semester that I have had dealing with folks who think that they are better than me, I have just become a little bit tougher. Going to college has made me tougher than living in the projects, and you know that's a shame. Educated Negroes are a trip! It's as if sistahs are sizing me up. I just went off on one chick and said, 'What the heck are you looking at? I must be big and beautiful because you can't keep your eyes off me.' "

"Well, you know we aren't like that," I said to her.

"I know, but it's hard to come down off of that."

"What about school? Are you able to keep up?" Rain asked Dymond.

Dy responded, "Yeah, I can keep up. What about you guys?"

Rain said that things were fine for her. I kept silent. I was glad to know that the two of them were doing well academically, but my situation was different in so many ways.

"You're kind of quiet, Payton," Dymond said. "That means it must be a little hard up there at UGA. Are you studying?"

"I am, but I have got an F. I haven't even told my mama. I have got to bring it up."

"You'd better bring it up, or you won't be driving ever again," Dymond said.

"My dad already took my car away after the accident. If I wanna drive, I have to get my grades up."

"That's a trip! Payton Skky has to walk. You've been driving since you were twelve."

"Eleven," I boasted.

We all laughed.

"Your boy has got a lot of cars here," Rain said as she looked around.

"Yeah, some of the cars have Georgia tags," I said. "He must have invited some people from the team. I don't see his roommate's car."

"Who's his roommate?" Dymond asked from the backseat.

As we parked and got out I said, "It's Tad, girl."

"Whaaat? I'm surprised they're both still alive," Dymond added, trying to be funny.

"C'mon in, ladies," Dakari said. "Thanks for bringing the grub, Pay."

"What do you want me to do with it, baby?" the eerie voice of Starr Love said from behind him.

Why did Dakari have to do that? Why did he invite me over when he already had female company? He knew that was wrong, and I didn't appreciate it. I rolled my eyes at him as Dymond and Rain walked into the house. I was in no rush to go in. I wanted to know what was up with Starr.

"Payton, aren't you coming in?" she asked me as though she really cared.

"I need to talk to him," I replied.

Starr stated in a sultry tone, "Don't be too long. The game is about to start, and I plan to massage my baby's back while he watches it."

I wanted to call her some of everything, but I knew I had to hold back my words.

178

As she switched away, Dakari said, "What's up?"

"Why did you invite me over here when you knew she was coming?"

"I didn't know she was coming until after I had called you. She called me, and I thought it was rude not to invite her. Why do you care anyway? I thought we were—what's that word you like to use?—friends," he replied, getting under my skin.

"I'm going to say this one time and one time only . . . " I started.

But before I could finish Starr pranced back over and kissed Dakari on the jaw. She tried tugging him away. "Kickoff is about to start. C'mon."

"I'll be there in a minute," he said as he patted her on the behind.

She giggled like a girl with no brains and walked away. She was just looking for someone to take the place of her dad and take care of her. No wonder she wasn't in school. I couldn't believe Dakari couldn't see that.

"Payton, what do you have to say? The game is about to begin."

"Dakari, we *are* friends, but there is still something there. Every time I say that I don't wanna be with you, you get mad and throw one of your little women in my face. I didn't come over here to see you hugged up with Starr. That's not right, and you know I don't do you like that."

"Yeah, right! I heard about you and Randall."

"Did you see anything? No, you were too busy with Shanay somewhere. I'm not one to spread gossip, but, after you, she went back to the party and got with Randall. There is something about the character of the women you are with these days. You had better be careful before you get something you can't get rid of."

I scooted past him quickly and sat by my girls. Frustration was running through my veins. Dakari sat on the floor as

Starr put her legs around him and started massaging his back like she said she was going to.

I had to think about whether I was going to let this get to me or whether I was going to be bigger than this. Maybe this was the only way I was going to get over him. He was such a dog! How could he care about me and let me witness him with another? After about three plays, I realized I was crazy to be sitting there watching Dakari and Starr. I hadn't talked to my girls in a long time, and I hadn't seen my aunts in even longer. I had tons of other things to do than to mess around in Dakari's world.

"Are y'all ready?" I asked.

"Yep," Rain quickly said.

Dymond blabbed, "Let me see this next play."

"C'mon," I said to Dymond.

"Why are y'all leaving?" someone from the football team said. "The party's about to get started. Don't you go to UGA?"

"Daaang!" another one said to me. "You are fine."

Though I appreciated the compliment, he could have kept it, because I was not in the mood.

We walked out of the door. Part of me wanted Dakari to follow us. However, thinking those thoughts let me know that I wasn't getting over him. I wasn't only supposed to leave in body but mentally too. I was no longer going to be caught up in Dakari's web of deception. Tad put it plainly: How can I care about a guy that is such a jerk?

Two days later, I sat with my brother and my father watching Georgia play. I was elated to see Dakari fumble as he was about to score on a kickoff return.

"Yeah!" I yelled aloud as my family looked at me as if I were crazy.

It might have been bad for me to be happy during Dakari's

disappointment. Since he didn't care about my feelings, I didn't care about his. However, when the fumble resulted in the other team getting a touchdown, the momentum seemed to leave Georgia and switch to Auburn. The Bulldogs were in trouble.

Eight minutes left in the game, and those minutes passed quickly as Auburn's running back did a long drive that ate up the clock. When we lost, I knew Dakari was going to hear it from his coaches and teammates. Not treating others as bad as I had been treated was a test that I had failed. I was ashamedly happy it was his fault. I knew this was going to devastate him.

"What's going on with you, Payton?" my dad asked. "I thought Dakari was your friend, and now you're taking pleasure in his pain. That doesn't seem like my daughter."

I wanted to let him know all of the mess Dakari had put me through, but I knew I couldn't.

"Sorry, Dad."

The Sunday after Thanksgiving, I was back in Athens sitting in the cafeteria for lunch. I only had a week and a half before I had to go back home for Christmas break. I needed to make my way to the library and buckle down to make up for my bad grades. Just as I looked down, I saw a twenty on the floor in front of me. I could use that money, but clearly it wasn't mine. I quickly looked across the room to see if anyone was looking for it. I didn't see anyone, so I quietly picked up the cash, and to my surprise it was four twenties—eighty dollars. It obviously had my name written all over it.

No sooner had I put the money in my pocket than I saw a redheaded guy whose brain was scurrying around like a mouse looking for cheese. I knew what he was searching for, but he didn't know that I knew. My feet wanted to dash out of the cafeteria with the money in my pocket, but my spirit wouldn't let me do that. I went up to him and asked him if he was looking for money. Sure enough, he was looking for eighty dollars. It was his. Probably, he could even tell me what serial number each twenty had.

"You dropped it back there," I told him, pointing to my table.

"I was eating there. God bless you. I'm from Arkansas, and my mom just wired me the money for my bus ticket home. Thank you."

The guy, who hadn't introduced himself to me, galloped away with a smile. I helped to make someone's day. That felt great.

"Thank You, Holy Spirit," I uttered aloud.

Though I wasn't richer financially, I was richer spiritually. I hadn't gone looking for the money, and I shouldn't have battled within to keep it. However, through all the doubts and uncertainties, in the end I did the right thing and grew from the experience.

"Basically, what I have learned from *The Color Purple*," I said to my literature teacher as I gave my oral presentation, "was that Miss Celie had to figure out what was holding her back from her dreams. In the end, she learned that it was herself. When she broke free of herself, she was able to stand up to all the other things that were trying to take control. Joy came, peace came, and love came."

Ms. Bissett asked me, "How can you relate to the story, or can you relate at all?"

"I know that for the four months I have been in college, it has been tough. It seems as if one thing after another has gone wrong. I blamed everyone but me for those incidents.

I then decided to become an overcomer, and I realized that I needed to study longer and harder and get help when I needed it. Without buckling down, I just wasn't measuring up. Now I think that I am doing better, and I have learned the same lesson as the one in the novel. I can achieve all of the things that I am capable of."

"That's a good lesson. I see you got the point of the story. If you use that principle in your life, you will be successful."

The class clapped.

Ms. Bissett told me that I was going to receive an A. I was thrilled because that would bring my grade up to a B. Now I just needed to do well on the rest of my exams.

"Am I over him or not?" I asked myself when I saw Tad standing across the street as I walked from one class to another.

My frame zoomed in so closely that I saw him hand in hand with that Vonda girl. They were laughing. *About what?* I wondered.

"I must care about you," I uttered, "because it is so good to see you smile, even if I am not the cause of it."

I stared so hard that I didn't realize they were walking toward me. What was I going to say?

"Payton, it's good to see you," Tad said as he reached out to hug me.

Without hesitation, I hugged him back. I peered over at Vonda and smiled cunningly. What was all that for? Just a second ago I was happy that she could make him happy. Now I was turning on her. Tad wasn't mine, and I needed to realize that.

She kindly smiled at me to let me know that she didn't read more into the hug than what was there. The next slick move she made was sliding her hand into his. He didn't step back from that.

Anger shot through my veins. What right did I have to feel that way? None.

"Can I talk to you for a minute?" I asked Tad.

He turned to Vonda and said, "I'll be back in one second."

"Sure," she said nicely.

"What's up, Payton?" he said as we stood a few feet from his new girl.

I began to interrogate him. "Are you guys dating? Do you like her better than me?"

"Are you jealous? I blame myself for our relationship not working out. When we first got together, I remember giving you a Christian book on dating. We finished that book, and it was great. We should have continued studying things of the Bible. Instead we focused on life issues. Though we prayed, I didn't lead the way I was supposed to. We fell off because the relationship wasn't built on any foundation. It says in James 1:19–20, 'Everyone should be quick to listen, slow to speak and slow to become angry, for man's anger does not bring about the righteous life that God desires. Therefore, get rid of all moral filth and the evil that is so prevalent and humbly accept the word planted in you, which can save you.' "

How could I argue with that? Tad wasn't answering my question; he was telling me how to be a better person with or without him. The Lord is not pleased when things of the world are more important than Him. God wanted me to keep myself pollutant free from the world, and Tad was try-ing to help clean me up.

I felt dejected but encouraged at the moment. We jour-neyed back over to Vonda. She was smiling at me.

She simply said, "Are you doing well on your exams? Are you passing your tests?"

Since Thanksgiving I'd had trial after trial, and test after test. Some I did well on, others I barely passed, and some I needed to try again. I couldn't answer her question. I remem-bered in James where it said, "The testing of your faith develops perseverance."

184

I wasn't the Christian that I needed to be, but because of Christ I could get better. I could pass the test I had failed before. I could fall but get up. I could do the right thing. Whatever came next I had determined I'd be passing whichever test.

14

Putting Up Decorations

$\mathcal{G}$ irl, why are you putting that wreath on the door?" I asked Laurel with a puzzled look on my face. "We are going home for Christmas in two days."

"I just wanted the room to have some Christmas cheer."

"Are you gonna take it down when we go home?"

"No, I was thinking I would leave it up," she told me. "Maybe the wreath would give our room some warmth for when we get back from vacation. How does it look? Is it straight?"

Though the wreath was tilted a little, I didn't see what difference it made. But it mattered to Laurel, and I had learned to support other people's issues and care about what they cared about. I fixed it without saying a word.

"Thanks, Payton. That looks really good. I'm going to miss you," she said with emotion.

I hadn't thought about it, but I would miss her too.

Laurel offered, "Payton, I know you are coming up to Conyers. Do you want to come by and spend the night over my house?"

I was shocked that she asked me. I had never spent the night over at a white girl's house. Laurel was cool, but the thought of staying with her was not one that I was in a rush to tackle.

She sensed something was wrong. "What? You're hesitating. What's wrong? I understand that you are staying with your grandmother, and I don't want to take that time away from you. Hey, maybe you could come over for dinner and a movie. We've got a brand-new movie theater. You could meet my friends."

"I'm sure it wouldn't be a problem. It would just be different for me."

"You've never spent the night over at someone's house?" she asked naively.

"Yes, but I've never stayed over a white person's house before. Have you ever stayed over a black girl's house?"

"Of course. I stayed over at my girlfriend's house from high school, and she stayed over mine. It was cool."

Laurel and I had talked, but I never knew she had a black friend. That was interesting. I wondered if they were really close. However, I didn't want to pry. I had no close white girlfriends, until now.

"I've got your number and you've got mine, so just call me. It will be a blast," she said, placing her hand on my shoulder.

"Thanks for the invite. I'm going to head up to the library. I've only got one more exam, and I'm going to blow it out of the water, and then I'm out of here on Tuesday."

There was a weird knock on our door. It was somewhat irritating. Laurel patiently opened the door. It was Jewels, just dying to be obnoxious, which she was whenever she opened her mouth.

Sarcastically she uttered, "Don't you think it's a little late to be putting up the Christmas stuff? We're about to go home, and there will be no one in the dorm to see it. This is stupid."

With a sweet spirit, Laurel replied, "I'm just hanging it up because Christ's birth is important."

"Whatever. Christmas just means that Santa Claus is coming, and it's time to update my wardrobe."

This chick had issues, and everyone knew it but her. Jewels thought she was better than everybody. As I looked at her with pity, I silently prayed that she would come to know Christ. Maybe one day she would let Christ into her heart.

As I headed out of the dorm, I saw Cammie. She looked upset.

"Girl, what are you doing here?" I pried. "I thought you were supposed to be on the campus Internet date. Tell me what's up? Was he lying over the computer?"

"The date started out great. We had nice conversation. I thought he liked me. I liked him. He was everything he said he was. He told me that I wasn't everything he thought I was."

"What!"

"He told me that I was too big-boned."

"He told you that you were big-boned?"

"His exact words were, 'Cammie, you are a lot bigger than I thought you'd be. I don't want someone who looks like that walking beside me. I'm sorry; you are just not what I want.'"

I didn't know what to say. I bet he wasn't all that because, if he was, then he would not have been surfing for a date on the Internet. He didn't have to down my friend like that.

I just threw my arms around her and said, "Girl, it's all right. He probably wasn't no good for you anyway."

"Payton, we had been talking on-line for the past two months. We had a connection, and now it's gone because of me."

188

She jerked away from me. Swiftly, she ran inside. I was so sad for her. I wanted to go after her, but I stood still. I figured she wanted to be alone. So I prayed for her instead. The Lord could give her the comfort I couldn't.

Lord, I pray for Cammie right now. Give her confidence, so that she can think she is beautiful. She is beautiful. Heal her heart. Amen.

I had finished all of my exams. I didn't know my grades yet, but I didn't care. It was time for me to go home and enjoy my friends and family. However, I still had to get presents for Cammie and Laurel before I left.

Buying presents was such a hard thing, but if I took my time and found what was symbolic, then I knew they would appreciate their gifts. I first had to call up my credit-card company to find out whether I still had room on my card. It would be easy to get something for my family.

Before I could get Cammie and Laurel's presents, I thought about Tad and Dakari. However, I quickly dismissed the thought. I just needed to shop for the girls, and if there was any time left, then I would possibly find something for Dakari and Tad.

Every store I passed was decorated in the most precious Christmas decor. The stores were just gorgeous. The Christian bookstore had a lovely tree. It wasn't just beautiful, but spectacular. It let me know that decorating meant pouring your heart out to Christ and praising Him and thanking Him. No present would come close to the gift of His life. Christ lives in the presence of His people. Seeing this, I just couldn't wait to get home and help Mom decorate our tree.

I started to get frustrated because I had done more window-shopping than actual buying. I had a budget, and I had to get gifts for Laurel, Cammie, Lynzi, Dymond, and

Rain. My list was getting extremely long, and I was so over-whelmed.

I ended up sitting up on a bench in the mall, extremely pressed for time. I had no idea what to get. Before me was a small store that sold clocks and things. The thought of having something engraved was very appealing.

All semester, we had been struggling with how we looked and felt about ourselves. I saw this cute little silver mirror and thought of the evil queen in Snow White asking who was the fairest of them all . . . it then replied to me, "You, Payton Skky, you are the fairest of them all. You've got it goin' on."

"Oh, this is so cute. I could put each person's initials on the back with the phrase 'Believe in what you see,' " I uttered aloud.

I jotted down all of the initials of my friends and handed them to the lady. She said it would take her forty-five min-utes to engrave all of the mirrors. Because of the time, I couldn't get Tad and Dakari presents, but I wasn't pressed about it.

After forty-five minutes, I grabbed my presents and caught a cab back to the dorm. When I looked into the bag I was slightly disappointed. Though all the gifts were there, they were just wrapped in plain white paper. They needed some sprucing up. I wanted the presentation to be perfect.

"Sir, could you pull into Eckerd Drugs for a second?" I asked the taxi driver.

"Sure, no problem."

Within ten minutes I was back in the cab. I had gotten some shiny teal green and cranberry red ribbon. Now my presents were pretty.

With all the stuff in hand, I had trouble opening my room door. Laurel must have heard me fidgeting with the door because she opened it before I could. One of her hands was behind her back.

"I got you something," she replied sweetly.

"I got you something, too," I replied, laughing.

We had such a great connection. She was such a cool person. Once again I was thankful God had placed her in my life as a roommate.

"It's good to see a smile on your face," I said to her as I sat down on my bed.

"It's been tough. Not bumping into Branson was a good thing. I have prepared myself to know that even if I did, I wouldn't fall head over heels. I owe that to you."

"No, girl, don't give me any credit. You believed in God and who He made you to be. You believed that God has a plan for your life that likely doesn't include Branson. Because you believed that, healing started to take place."

"Yeah, but enough of Branson. Besides, all the stuff that we went through, I was crazy to still like him anyway. I hope I see you in Conyers."

"I'm planning to talk to my mom about it on the way back to Augusta. It would be good to stay with you."

"OK, what did you get me?" she asked. "Here, open mine."

She handed me a box wrapped in gold paper. I couldn't wait to unwrap it. Actually, I tore it open.

"This is so sweet," I said to her as I saw the new pages for my Franklin planner.

"I remember you told me that you had gotten one last year as a debutante. I got these pages at the Christian bookstore, and it has daily Scriptures to inspire you. I am not as organized as you, but I think the planner made a big difference because when I slacked off in the beginning of the semester, it was no fun. Things definitely got better when I started giving God back His time."

Moments later, she was very happy when she saw her gift. "I've been told that I was cute all my life, but deep down I questioned it."

I encouraged, "Well, as it says, believe in what you see."

"I'm going to start doing that. Thanks, Payton."

I told Laurel that, if my mom came, to tell her that I would be right back. After knocking on Cammie's door, I was disappointed because it seemed as if she had already gone. When I started to walk away, Cammie opened the door.

"Hey, I thought you were already gone," I bounced up to her and said.

"No, I don't leave until in the morning," she replied sadly.

As I handed her the box, I replied, "Well, I'm about to leave, but I wanted to give this to you."

"Payton, this is so sweet. You didn't have to get me anything. I didn't get you anything."

"That's OK. I wanted to do it. I expect nothing, girl. Your friendship has been enough."

"Come on in," she said.

I could tell Cammie was still down from the day before. I had been praying for her, but her puffy eyes let me know that I needed to pray some more. She was still very out of it.

"Girl, I hope you didn't spend a lot of money on me," she said as she opened the present slowly.

I said, "Don't worry about it."

"The mirror is really pretty, but I don't really like looking at myself. I don't look like you."

"What does that mean?"

"It means you're cute, and I'm not."

"You're cute, Cammie," I said, getting tired of her putting herself down.

"Looking in the mirror is just a horrific sight."

"Flip it over, Cammie. Read it."

Carefully she read, "Believe in what you see."

"Now turn it over . . . I see a beautiful girl who is extremely smart."

Tears started streaming down her face. This was hard.

They were sad tears, but in the midst of them, I could see her getting encouraged.

When I looked at the clock and saw that my mom was soon to arrive, I hugged her and told her I would be praying for her.

"Thanks, Payton."

I should have known that my mom would have been there early. When I opened the door, I was happy to see her carrying on a conversation with Laurel's mom. It was the first time our moms had met.

Laurel and I stepped into the bathroom.

I joked, "Maybe I'll have to bring my mom to spend the night, too. It seems as though she has made a new friend."

"Yeah, they really seem to be enjoying each other," Laurel responded. "I hope you don't mind, but I have already told Mother that I invited you over. She said she'd be happy to have you."

"Girls," we heard my mother call.

We said our good-byes and locked up the room.

"So, it seems you're getting along with your new roommate," my mom said on the drive home.

"Yeah, it was weird at first, but I like her."

"I'm glad you have stepped out of your comfort zone and found this to be a good experience."

I really liked it when I could talk to her like she was not only a mom but also a friend. I could tell she wanted to ask me something.

"What is it, Mom?"

"What about Tad and Dakari? How was your semester with them?"

I really didn't want to go there. So I turned up the music. She didn't bug me. We sang Christmas carols most of the way home.

After we got back to Augusta, we hung up the lights and ate pizza. We were still an artificial-tree family, and I liked that because I hated to get stuck by pine needles.

"You're quite the helper this year," my mom said to me.

"I know. I have a different appreciation for it. I realized I took a lot of things for granted, including you. Putting up decorations should be a gift back to God for all that He has done for us."

"Well, that's a revelation to me," my mom responded. "What a great perspective. Everyone needs to hear that. Awesome! You're right . . . it's the least we could do for all God did for us by giving us His only Son."

There we stood, arm in arm, in an embrace that was long anticipated. God had given me another special gift. Not only had I learned that I needed to praise Him in all that I do, but I realized that if I listened to the wisdom of my mother, I would have it going on.

"Y'all are slackin'," my brother said as he came into the room with my dad.

"Yeah," my dad agreed, teasing. "Y'all are a trip. Hugging when y'all are supposed to be putting up decorations."

15

Loving
Every Part

"ᴘayton, are you asleep?" my dad peeked into my room and asked on the night of my return.

I wasn't doing anything but listening to *A Soulful Christmas* CD.

"I'm awake, Dad. Come in."

"I'm proud of you, Payton."

I thought to myself, *You haven't seen my grades yet. Don't be too proud,* but I hoped that my last-minute efforts would prove to be successful.

My dad stated, "I just wanted to tell you I missed you. It's nice to peek into your room and see you in here. I've been praying for you."

"I missed you too, Dad."

"Since it's not that late, how about a game of Chinese checkers? Plus, I want to give you one of your gifts a little early. Your mom is almost finished wrapping it."

A grin spread across my face as I jumped out of bed. Chinese checkers was our game. We had played it ever since

I was little. I ran downstairs to the beautifully decorated family room and started setting up the marbles.

My dad entered with a bowl of popcorn and said, "All right, I'm gonna beat you."

"Talk is cheap," I replied.

Halfway through the game, he had two more marbles to get to the other side. Somehow, someway, I jumped him and won. I was loving every minute of it. We were both fiercely competitive.

"Don't get mad 'cause I beat you," I teased.

Mom had three elegantly wrapped presents in her arms. She bent over, and my dad took the one off the top. She stood behind the couch and in front of the crackling fire. She was smiling, and so was my dad. Something was up.

"Baby girl, this is a gift for you from me."

The box was so light. However, it wasn't a small box. I had no clue what was in it.

"Do I open it now?" I asked.

"No, you already have what's inside. You're just supposed to keep the box and look at it when you need to."

I chuckled. "I'm confused, Daddy. What's inside?"

"Self-confidence. Now you've got it just like you asked . . . wrapped, neatly in a box. Every time you see it, know you're just like it . . . a pretty package with self-confidence locked inside."

That was a strong statement and the best gift I'd never open. I hugged my dad. My mother smiled and went upstairs to get ready for bed.

Perry had taken his girlfriend out on a date. He was just returning. He came through the front door, and he didn't seem happy.

"Did you have fun?" I asked.

"Yeah, it was all right."

"I've got the Chinese checkerboard out, and I just beat Dad. Do you wanna play?"

"Where's Mama?"

"She's upstairs getting ready for bed. She'll be down in a second. Do you wanna play?"

"Yeah, set up marbles for all of us."

That was going to be so much fun. We played three more times, and I didn't win any of them. My family taunted and teased me. I told them we would have a rematch another night, and they all would lose.

The next night we sat at the table to play a different game—spades. My family loved spades. It was Dad and me against Perry and Mom. We were going to cheat. It was against God's principles, but my brother and mother knew we were going to cheat, so that made it fun.

As we were getting our strategy together, Dad said, "Tomorrow is the dealership's annual Christmas party. This year, since I'm allowing Perry to bring a date, you can bring one, too."

"Dad, that's not fair. I didn't get to bring a date when I was Perry's age. This double-standard thing is ridiculous," I joked with a bit of seriousness.

The sit-down dinner in the middle of the showroom was always great. It was an all-around good time. The thought of bringing a date was somewhat appealing, but who? Tad now had a girlfriend, and Dakari was out of the picture.

As I held a handful of spades, I thought back over the years when we used to do this. It was magical. It seemed like I had the best family on earth.

"Thanks, Lord," I mouthed. "Thanks for this blessing."

We were playing until a team reached 250 points. My father and I were twenty-five points away from winning when my telephone rang. I dashed to my room.

"Hey, Payton."

"Tad?" I said, shocked.

"Yep. It's me. How are you doing? Are you busy?"

"No," I said, even though I heard my dad and brother calling me from downstairs.

"I hear someone calling you."

"We're having some family time. Do you mind if I call you back?"

"Yeah, go ahead. I'll be home."

"OK; I'll hit you back in a few."

When I went back to the table, I didn't realize that I was smiling noticeably. I got called out.

"So, what guy was on the phone? You're already setting up your date for tomorrow night, huh?" my dad asked.

I had forgotten all about the party. I could only think about Tad calling me. At that point, the game meant nothing.

"Payton, I can't believe you let them beat us," my dad said after we finished.

"I know, dang," I joked back. "I've got a call to make. We will get them back later, Dad."

I was so excited. Though I had no rationality as to why, I was. Quickly I called Tad back, and the line was busy. However, I pressed redial and gratefully I got through with no problem.

"Hey, are you asleep?" I asked.

"No, I was just waiting on you to call."

"What's up?"

"I just wanted to know if your family wanted to go to a game with me on New Year's."

"I'll ask them. I'm sure they would."

"I know that your dad and brother like football, so I thought I would ask."

"That's so sweet."

My dad came into my room and said, "Are you talking to Tad?"

After I had answered yes, he took the phone and started talking. "Hey, Tad, has Payton asked you to the dealership

198

Christmas party yet? Yeah, it's tomorrow night. You don't need a tux; just wear a suit. We'd love to see you there. Well, I'll see you later."

"Dad!" I said as I grabbed the phone back. "I'm sorry, Tad."

"No, it's OK. So, it looks as if I am going to a party tomorrow night."

"Is it OK?" I asked him timidly.

"Yeah, I appreciate the invite. Do I need to come by your house to pick you up?"

"Yeah, be here at about seven."

"OK, I'll see you tomorrow night."

"Bye."

As I laid back on my bed I wondered, *What is going to happen tomorrow?*

As I sat and got my nails done at my old salon, I realized how much I missed the days of primping. I loved getting my hair and nails done. I had been roughing it in college.

"Are you going somewhere special, or are you doing this for Christmas?" my old friend asked as she buffed my nails.

"I've got a date."

"Oooh, tell me about it, girl."

I responded shyly, "It's no big deal."

"I didn't ask if it was a big deal. I asked you to tell me about it."

"My dad's dealership is having its Christmas party. I'm going with Tad."

"That's the boy who took you to your debutante ball. He's cute. You go, girl!"

"I think he likes someone else, and my dad kind of cornered him into taking me. So don't make too much of it."

"Don't even go there, because Tad is a grown man. If he

199

didn't want to go then he would have gotten out of it."

"You're right. He did sound a little excited. So make me pretty."

"You're already pretty. You've just got to believe it."

"I'm starting to."

"Good for you."

As soon as I was getting ready to leave, Miss Shirley, Tyson's mom, stopped me and said, "You know my son has got a new girlfriend."

I don't know why, but Tyson's mom never really liked Rain. What was she talking about? Hopefully she had the wrong information. I needed to call Rain, but she was at her grandmother's house until Christmas. So I didn't make too much of Miss Shirley's comment.

"I love that dress. You're looking nice," my brother said, twirling me around.

"Are you going to pick up your date and meet us there?" I asked.

"Yep, that's the plan," he said, walking out of the door as Tad walked in.

"You look lovely," were the first words that came out of my date's mouth.

It had been a while since we had seen each other. I wanted to ask him about Vonda, but I didn't want to ruin the evening. I was going to have to trust God, relax, and not stress.

As I noticed Tad continually checking me out, I smiled back to let him know I appreciated it. We were quiet most of the way there, but it wasn't a bad quiet. It was a peaceful and serene feeling.

As we arrived at our destination, even more joy entered into the equation as we saw the lovely decorations. The showroom floor looked like a hotel ballroom. There was a five-piece band playing Christmas music, which made the most heavenly sound.

"Are you sitting with your dad?" Tad asked.

"Yeah, we're sitting at the head table."

"Which one is the head table? They all look so nice," he joked.

"Are you OK sitting with my family?"

"Yeah, I've brushed up on my etiquette. I won't mess up like last time," he said, laughing.

I remember when Tad had first come over for dinner. He was so nervous that he drank my dad's tea instead of his. Tonight he seemed so polished. He was such a gentleman.

"So, how has this semester been for you?" he asked.

"It hasn't been the best. My suite mate tried to kill herself."

"Is she OK?"

"Yeah, she's back. Before that, Worth Zachary was killed. It's been a crazy semester."

We didn't get to finish catching up because the evening started. It was full of celebration. This was a Christian business, and this celebration was a Christian one, because if Jesus hadn't been born then we wouldn't have any hope.

My dad grabbed the mike and said, "For unto us a child is born. For unto us a Son is given. I thank you all for what you have done to put this dealership on the map. This is a great occasion to celebrate and be joyous. When we seek God first, blessings come down. Jesus loved us so much that He gave His life so that we could have eternal life. Enjoy your evening and your holiday season."

We were dancing, and the way Tad looked at me was so special and captivating that I knew he cared deeply.

"What are you smiling about?" I asked.

"I'm just counting my blessings. My birthday is in a couple days, and I will be nineteen years old. I have been blessed over my nineteen years. I'm thankful because I have been blessed with riches from the heart. Therefore, I am able to appreciate a pretty girl. It's a blessing."

"What are you talking about?"

"I think a lot of you, Payton. I was sad when things didn't work out between us. God was so good that He allowed me to fall back in love with Him. To feel those feelings is a blessing, and I won't take them lightly. I never thought I could feel for a girl what I felt for you. When that was destroyed, a part of me was, too."

We were dancing, and I wanted to cry. Tad was so real and so special. How in the world did I mess this up? As he talked about spiritual things, I was able to understand that this wasn't about us. How awesome and special was his walk with Christ. That's how Tad believes in himself, because he knows who he is in Christ. That was my problem. I was still trying to be the captain of my own ship.

Later in the car as Tad took me home, I said, "The joy that you have now is what I'm striving to get. I wanna be so in love with God that nothing else in the world matters. I'm not there yet, but I wanna get there."

"Having the desire to get there is the first step. I thought I was there, but I realized that too many times I was concerned with things of the world instead of being concerned with things of the Spirit. Christ can be all you need and more. I challenge you to try it. Let the Lord surprise you."

"Why do you say that?"

"Because I think that part of you feels that you couldn't be complete with just Him alone."

"How did you know?"

"I was there, Payton. I was angry, and I was bitter when things didn't work out my way. God has plans for all of our lives. He knows it all. Just because things don't work out at that time doesn't mean that they won't work out. Sometimes when things don't work out, it's better."

"Do you mean us?" I asked him.

He gently caressed my face with the hand that wasn't on the steering wheel and breathed sincerely, "I loved being your boyfriend. I don't know what's going to happen. I don't know where things are going with Vonda and me, but she's my sister in Christ first, and I really like that."

"I understand," I told him. "I've given you a hard time about her, but she's a cute girl, and she seems to care deeply for you. I hope it works out."

By that time we were at my front door. His last words were, "Not really sweatin' it, but maybe it will. But, hey, I'll be praying that you get a love for Christ that exceeds anything else."

"Thanks," I told him. "I need that. And thanks for making tonight . . . a Christmas dream."

We hugged. It was an embrace that said good night, but it also felt like good-bye. This was hard to accept. However, I realized I had brought this on myself. Tad was a great person, and I didn't need to block his blessings any longer.

As he drove off, I prayed, *Lord, take care of him.*

The next day, which was three days before Christmas, I called my girls. Lynzi's mom said she wasn't coming home until Christmas Eve. I told her to let Lynzi know that I'd be waiting to see her. Rain still hadn't gotten back from her grandmother's house, but Dymond was home.

"Hey, girl!"

"Payton! What's up?"

"You sound better. During Thanksgiving you were kind of mean."

"Don't hold it against a sistah; it was the stress. I got all A's."

"That is great."

"I love it at Howard. It's different, but once I learned that I was who I was and that was not going to change, I was proud of that . . . things went great. My mom is calling me. We're about to go shopping. I'll call you later. I'm out."

Later that evening, I started reflecting on my life that semester. I grabbed my jacket and decided to walk the neighborhood. I had my Discman in my coat and was listening to Yolanda Adams, and her lyrics consumed my soul.

Have you ever felt distraught, yet overjoyed, broken up, yet completely together, or wounded, yet as good as new? Well, that was how I felt all semester, that is, until I realized that where I lacked, Christ was sufficient. I was sad that I was a sinner, but I was happy because God sent His only Son to change all of that.

I was broken by the Holy Spirit that had finally won the battle with my flesh. To love God couldn't be a haphazard thing—one day walking with God, the next doing more talking than walking.

I started getting caught up in what it means to praise God. I was free. I was so thankful that I knew that deep inside, at that moment, I truly loved God. Tears were pouring from my eyes. I had a hunger for holiness.

In my mind as I was weeping, angels were drying my tears. I could feel them blowing new life into my old, tired body. Telling me that I was somebody because I was a child of the King.

Stand tall, Payton, echoed through my heart, like the heart of a brave soldier going to war.

The indigo sky that my heavenly Father created was romancing me like I'd never been romanced before. The wind was whispering in my ear and sending kisses that made me lose my breath. The stars were winking at me and telling me I was beautiful.

Then in that moment of silence and perfection, God said, *Payton . . . I did all this because I love you. Now can you see I am enough?*

I sat down on the ground and continued crying because I loved God so much. He was enough. I loved Christ, and I could be anything because He made me something.

"Thank You, Lord," I said as I raised my hand to the clear, dark night. "Thank You for making a Payton Skky. Thank You for making and loving me."

I realized that through this whole year, I'd been struggling with self-acceptance. I'd not been trusting God for who He made me to be. So many times, by my words and actions, I'd basically said to God, "What You've given me is not enough! I want to be smarter, prettier, more talented." Now I know that kind of thinking is wrong. I'd been implying God made mistakes when He made me. *Forgive me, Lord,* I prayed. *I know that accepting myself is not a cop-out. I now embrace me.*

I didn't know what tomorrow would hold, but, as the song said, one day I would leave this earthly dwelling. I couldn't do anything about the past, but from this second forward, I didn't have to have any more regrets. Never would I forget that I have self-worth, not because of who I am, but because my worth is in Christ.

I was determined to make the best of the rest of my days. I was determined to live my life to the fullest. I realized my very existence was a gift from God, and I was determined to start loving every part.

Staying Pure #1

Payton Skky has everything a high school senior would want--popularity, well-to-do parents, and excellent grades. To top that off, she dates the most sought after boy in her school, Dakari Graham. However, when Dakari puts on the pressure to take their relationship to the next level, Payton goes numb. Torn between what her soul believes and what her heart wants, she struggles to make the best decision. Will her choice be the right one?

ISBN: 0-8024-4236-6, Paperback

Sober Faith #2

Payton Skky just had the night of her life-- introduced to society as a debutante with a bright future, and things were back on track with her new boyfriend and escort, Tad Taylor. However, when it comes time to celebrate, Payton's friends want to toast with something other than punch. Though she wants to be down with her girls, Tad warns her that the consequences could be severe. Which will win...the flesh or the Spirit?

ISBN: 0-8024-4237-4, Paperback

Saved Race #3

Payton Skky is about to accomplish a life-long dream- graduate from high school with honors. However, when Payton's gorgeous, biracial, cousin, Pillar Skky steps on the scene and Payton has to deal with feelings of jealousy and anger towards her. Though she knows God wants her to have a tight relationship with her cousin, years of family drama seem to keep them forever apart. Will Payton accept past hurts or embrace God's grace?

ISBN: 0-8024-4238-2, Paperback

Surrendered Heart #5

Payton Skky finally has her priorities straight; to live each moment for God. The legacy of her grandfather's life lets her know that in the end the only thing that will matter is knowing for certain that even though people may reject the message of salvation, she still needs to do her best to represent Christ.

Though she gets discouraged, her good friend Tad Taylor helps to keep her focused on carrying out God's commands. While the two of them try to mend their hearts back together, many things around them fall apart. Will they work out...or will things remain the same?

ISBN: 0-8024-4240-4 Paperback

MOODY
PUBLISHERS

THE NAME YOU CAN TRUST.

1-800-678-6928 www.MoodyPublishers.com

SWEETEST GIFT TEAM

ACQUIRING EDITOR:
Cynthia Ballenger

COPY EDITOR:
Chandra Sparks Taylor

COVER DESIGN:
Lydell Jackson

INTERIOR DESIGN:
Ragont Design

PRINTING AND BINDING:
Versa Press Incorporated

The typeface for the text of this book is
Berkeley